LESLIE BROOKS ELLIOT couldn't understand why Brad was avoiding her and acting as if he had lost all interest in her. Was her marriage over?

BRAD ELLIOT knew how much he was hurting Leslie, but it was unavoidable. He had to leave her before it was too late. How could he tie her down to him when he would soon be blind?

LANCE PRENTISS was dazzled by Leslie's beauty and talent. He would make her forget all about Brad—if she would only return his love.

———————————

Series Story Editor **Mary Ann Cooper** is America's foremost soap opera expert. She writes the nationally syndicated column *Speaking of Soaps*, is a major contributor to soap opera magazines and has appeared on numerous radio and television talk shows.

Charlotte Granville, author of *One Shining Moment*, spends half the year living in her loft in Manhattan. At other times she can be found in her palazzo in the hills of Bologna.

Dear Friend,

One of the nicest things about serving as Story Editor for Soaps & Serials books is the opportunity to read the wonderful letters I receive from our readers. It's gratifying to know how much you enjoy these books. At Pioneer we work with the finest romance authors and editors to produce books that recapture, relish, and relive the rich history of soap operas through the retelling of stories that have entertained millions of viewers over the years.

These books bring back precious memories of the past, but they also raise questions, too. A reader from Gary, Indiana, wrote us recently to ask where Genoa City is on THE YOUNG AND THE RESTLESS. The answer is that no one knows where Genoa City is located. It is a fictional town created by William and Lee Bell. Most soap opera settings are fictional, with the obvious exception of SANTA BARBARA. Also, RYAN'S HOPE makes no secret of the fact that it takes place in New York City.

For Soaps & Serials Books,

Mary Ann Cooper

Mary Ann Cooper

P.S. If you missed previous volumes of Soaps & Serials books and can't find them in your local book source, please see the order form inserted in this book.

The Young and the Restless

7
ONE SHINING MOMENT

William J. Bell and Lee Phillip Bell, Co-Creators,
Executive Producers, and Head Writers

PIONEER COMMUNICATIONS NETWORK, INC.

One Shining Moment

THE YOUNG AND THE RESTLESS paperback novels are published and distributed by Pioneer Communications Network, Inc.

SOAPS & SERIALS™ is a trademark of Pioneer Communications Network, Inc.

ISBN: 0-916217-77-9

Printed in Canada

10 9 8 7 6 5 4 3 2 1

ONE SHINING MOMENT

Chapter One
On Stage

The final brilliant chords of the Rachmaninoff concerto filled the large concert hall. Before the last note had died down, the entire audience was standing, cheering, "Bravo!"

Leslie Brooks-Elliot lifted her fingers from the piano and raised her head.

The applause increased. People began calling, "Encore!"

Leslie stood and turned to face them. Her luxuriant chestnut hair, caught up in a classical twist, gleamed under the spotlight. Her slender body, outlined by the long, clinging black crepe dress, appeared fragile and delicate. Her dark eyes shone, highlighted by the theatrical lights and the thin veil of happy tears that welled up in her eyes. She bowed her head slightly to the crowd.

Their cheering increased, and they began to throw flowers toward the stage. Long-stemmed red roses piled up at her feet. A beaming young usher, caught up in the excitement, came forward from the wings bearing an enormous bouquet and ceremoniously presented it to Leslie.

As she accepted the flowers graciously and smiled back at the audience, underneath the thrill of the moment, her thoughts flew back to the difficult period she had just lived through. Her breakdown. The slow, halting steps toward being able to face the world again. But now all that was behind her. All the pain, all the agony, all the torture and self-doubt —gone; all of it gone. She was strong again. She had survived a terrible ordeal, and now her whole life stretched out before her, filled with hope.

She bowed her head again to the crowd, and they called out enthusiastically, "Bravo! Encore! Encore!"

Leslie's eyes scanned the audience. She couldn't see far beyond the first few rows since the stage lights were so bright. Finally her eyes rested on her family, in the third row. Her mother looked elegant, beautiful and proud. Her father, handsome in his tuxedo, his distinguished gray hair gleaming, stood straight and tall, applauding and proud for his daughter. He caught her eye, raised his hand over his head, gave her the okay sign and winked. They exchanged a secret smile between them, and Leslie knew that he, too, was thinking how wonderful it was to see her so strong after all they'd been through.

Next to him stood Leslie's younger sister, Laurie. Like all the Brooks family, she, too, was beautiful. Her royal-blue sequined jacket sparkled. At that moment, Laurie was looking around the audience, craning her neck, as she clapped her hands absently and automatically. Leslie wondered whom her sister was searching for in the crowd.

Then Leslie turned her head toward the wings, and there, applauding harder than anyone, stood Brad. How handsome he looked, she thought. And how proud. How wonderful that he had stood by her through thick and thin, that he was always there for her, standing in the wings, waiting for her to come off the stage so that he could wrap her in his strong arms.

Brad mouthed the words, "I love you," and for one moment, the cheering crowd, the lights, the glittering gilt concert hall, the crystal chandeliers, the ladies in diamonds, furs and evening gowns, the men in tuxedos, the flowers—all of it faded into the background. Only Leslie and Brad existed, smiling at one another. They were husband and wife, lovers and friends, sharing a glorious moment as they shared all moments.

Leslie whispered back to Brad, "I love you, too."

With a gesture of his hand, he signaled her to turn back to her audience. She smiled at him once more and turned obediently.

Brad watched adoringly as she bowed again. He loved the delicate curve of her neck, the regal way she stood before the audience, accepting their applause. His heart was filled with love for his wife, who had made it through such a terrible ordeal.

The crew member who ran the lights backstage was an old-timer. He shouted to Brad over the roar of the crowd, "Boy, I've seen all the greats, but your wife really knows how to milk a crowd. She oughta give 'em an encore, though. They been beggin' for it enough."

Just at that moment, Leslie raised her hand to the audience. They shouted, "Encore!" even louder. The usher came forward to take Leslie's bouquet, and she took her place again at the piano.

The audience quickly settled back down in their seats as a hush filled the huge hall. Leslie sat for a moment, her hands in her lap, concentrating. Not a program rustled. Not a person moved. They sat, waiting, expectant.

Leslie's hands moved toward the piano, hovering for a split second. As she raised her hands dramatically to strike the first chord, the lights caught the diamond she wore on her left hand.

Brad saw the brilliant gleam from the ring he'd given her. But as he looked, something happened. The gleam became fuzzy. For one brief moment, it was as if everything were slowly being covered by a milky gray film. He blinked. He blinked again. His hand automatically reached out for something to support himself. He found the shoulder of the stagehand and held on.

The stagehand thought the handsome young husband was gripping his shoulder out of pride for his wife. The old-timer patted Brad's hand and whispered, "Yup, she's a real pro."

As fast as the moment had come, it was over, and everything came sharply back into focus for Brad. He breathed a sigh of relief.

He was overworked, he told himself. That was the reason he'd been having these moments of blurriness. He had to get more sleep.

He tried to listen to Leslie's sonata, but his pleasure was marred by the nagging thought that maybe it wasn't just that he was overtired. Maybe there was another reason for the fact that with increasing regularity, he was having trouble seeing.

Leslie woke slowly and from habit reached out for Brad. Her hand groped around his side of the bed until she finally woke up enough to realize that he was already gone. She glanced at the clock: 11:30. Stretching luxuriously, she allowed herself to lie in bed. This was the first morning in months that she hadn't gotten up early to practice.

The crisp autumn sun speckled its way through the branches of the tree outside their bedroom window and sent beautiful dapples of sunlight through the filmy curtains. Leslie's eyes strayed around their restful bedroom. Traces of last night's success were everywhere. Huge bouquets of flowers in vases sat all over the bureau and the bedstands. Telegrams from well-wishers were piled on the small writing desk. Her dress was slung carelessly over the chaise longue, and Brad's tux lay in a crumpled heap nearby. Their shoes and stockings left a trail that ended at the bed.

She smiled to herself, remembering how she and Brad, happier than they'd been in who knew how long, had kissed their way into the bedroom from the front door, each one helping the other off with their clothes, tossing them wherever they landed, until the two of them had fallen laughing into bed together.

Oh, Brad, she thought, *what would I ever do without you?*

After the concert in Chicago, they'd gone to a large congratulatory party. Hundreds of Chicago's finest citizens had been there, a sea of smiling faces around her, all leaning forward to compliment her and shake her hand.

She smiled as she remembered Brad whispering in her ear, "I wish I had a nickel for every one of them who said, 'Whoops! Better not shake your hand too hard.'"

They had toasted her. She had drunk champagne and eaten caviar and smoked salmon until the limousine had arrived to take her, Brad, and the rest of her family to the airport. Then they'd taken a small plane back to Genoa City. They hadn't reached home until almost five in the morning. She and Brad had finally drifted off to sleep, wrapped in each other's arms, at dawn.

But he must have been up early, Leslie thought. For on her bedside table lay a stack of Chicago newspapers, all open to the entertainment sections, with the reviews of her concert neatly circled in red. How considerate he always was.

She stretched again and swung her legs out of bed. As she padded barefoot across the thick carpet toward the bathroom, she thought how lucky she was. Lucky to be able to play music. Lucky to be in love. Lucky to have had such a success on her first concert of the new season. And most of all, lucky to be married to the most wonderful, handsome, honorable, considerate man in the whole world. Once more she wondered what she would ever do without him?

Brad parked his BMW and walked toward the Genoa City News Building. It was the kind of morning that made the whole world tingle with life. Leaves crackled underfoot. The sun shone brilliantly, and the rich, fragrant smell of fall was in the clean, invigorating air.

As he walked, Brad felt a sense of peace and exhilaration at the same time, as if now, on this beautiful day, in this beautiful season, his and Leslie's life had begun anew. Their troubles were behind them.

He allowed himself one silly moment from boyhood—he kicked a pile of leaves and delighted in the crackling sound they made, in the bright orange, yellow and deep red swirls as the leaves rose up and then settled back down on the ground.

His mind was humming with plans. He would write a series of pieces, one for each city of Leslie's tour. Perhaps he could do a series on luncheonettes. Or local radio stations. Something interesting for the readers of Genoa City, to show them a slice of life from each of the cities he visited. Suddenly he thought of the old stagehand last night. That was it! He could do a series of feature articles about one old-timer in each of the concert halls Leslie played. They must each have a hundred funny or sad stories to tell of all the famous musicians and performers they'd seen in their lives. Wonderful! He'd call it "Tales from Backstage."

But suddenly he remembered something else —that moment in the wings when he'd found his vision blurring. Maybe he should stop worrying and simply make an appointment with an eye doctor. He couldn't imagine why he hadn't thought of it before. That was all it was: he needed glasses. Must be getting old, he thought wryly. Well, glasses wouldn't be so bad. People almost expected journalists to wear glasses. Tortoiseshell frames would be appropriate.

He felt confident and sure again as he pushed through the revolving doors of the newspaper building and headed for the bank of elevators. At his floor, he got off and walked into the bustling newsroom.

"Hey, Brad!" People looked up from their typewriters and telephones. "Congratulations! Heard Leslie's concert was a huge success," they called out as he strode past the rows of desks.

Smiling, he called back, "Thanks. It was great!" Suddenly, he felt a stabbing pain behind his eyes and winced. His vision blurred. He blinked, and everything snapped back into focus again.

Don't panic, he told himself. Just make an appointment with an eye doctor.

He sat down at his desk and reached for the phone.

* * *

Laurie took another sip of coffee and tossed the newspaper onto the pile that already lay at her feet. Review after review raved on about her sister's performance. Sympathy, Laurie thought spitefully. Each and every one of those critics was writing out of sympathy. They all knew that Leslie had had a breakdown. They all knew it was a miracle she was playing again. That's all these reviews were, sympathy. Nothing more.

She picked up another newspaper, skimmed the review and tossed it onto the pile. It wasn't that she expected any reviews to have noticed her book. No, she knew better than that. They never reviewed sexy books. What galled her was that it hadn't sold. She would've liked nothing better than to have made oodles of money on that book. Then she wouldn't have to rely on her father.

Her father—hah! That was a laugh. Stuart Brooks wasn't even her real father. Although he didn't know that. But she knew. And it hurt her. It made her want to be free from the Brooks family forever.

Free from the shadow of delicate, fragile Leslie, whom everyone was always so solicitous about. Free from having to accept, on one family occasion after another, the fact that Brad only had eyes for Leslie and had never even given Laurie a tumble. And she wanted to be free from her mother, who had shared the secret of her own guilt and burdened Laurie with a truth she wished she'd never known.

Yes, she wanted to be free from it all. And what she wanted freedom from more than anything else was the horrible, burning ache of Mark's rejection. That he hadn't loved her as much as she loved him. She had tried so hard to convince him that their love could overcome any difficulty. If they were related by blood, she had argued, they could marry anyway and not have children. But no, Mark had rejected her. He'd said their love was dirty. Shame washed over her again as she recalled his words. But it wasn't her fault, she wanted to cry out loud for the whole world to hear. It wasn't her fault!

But she was condemned to silence for the sake of the family name. And so, she had to shoulder the burden of secrecy and remain silent.

There was one thing the family couldn't stop her from doing, though—making a name for herself as a writer. If she could do that, she'd be free from them all.

Pushing back from the breakfast table, she walked resolutely to her desk. She took out the folders of the book she was working on, slapped them on the desk and sat down at the typewriter with grim determination.

Stop moping, Laurie told herself. Get to work.

Soon, the sound of her typewriter clacking away at a furious rate traveled out the window of her apartment and into the crisp, fall air.

Brad burst through the doors of Stuart's office. Stuart looked up, mildly annoyed at the sound, but when he saw it was his son-in-law, he smiled.

"You're awfully chipper this morning," Stuart said. "That's one of the advantages of youth. You can be out until all hours of the morning, and show up bright-eyed and bushy-tailed for work the next morning. Me, I'm sitting here nursing a cup of coffee and trying to look busy, hoping my secretary won't catch me." He laughed heartily.

Brad laughed along with him. "Stuart," he began energetically, "I had a great idea this morning—"

"Whoa, whoa, hold your horses." Stuart motioned Brad into a chair. "Would you like some coffee?"

"Sure, thanks." Brad nodded, sitting down.

Stuart reached for his intercom and asked his secretary to bring in two cups. Then he settled back into his chair. "You know, Brad, I wanted to thank you for last night."

Brad raised his eyebrows. "Thank me? Why thank me? I just stood around like a stage-door Johnny."

Stuart's secretary came in carrying two steaming cups of coffee. "Oh, good morning, Brad," she said when she saw him. "Congratulations to you for Leslie's big success last night. Everybody's buzzing about it."

"Thank you." Brad accepted the coffee cup, and the secretary left. "Everyone's been so complimentary all morning," he said as he sipped his coffee. "You'd think I had something to do with it."

"Ah, but you did," Stuart said, and Brad detected a serious note in Stuart's voice that hadn't been there before. "I owe you a lot as Leslie's father," Stuart went on. "I don't really know if she'd have pulled through without you by her side."

Brad shifted uncomfortably in his chair. Compliments were something he'd never gotten used to accepting. "I think you're the one to thank, really, Stuart. She had her whole family behind her."

"That's nice of you to say, but fathers are sometimes the cause of problems, and husbands are often the cure."

"I don't think we should lay blame at anyone's door. Sometimes these things just . . . happen. You probably know better than I do that Leslie's fragile. Sometimes the world's just too hard for her to take. I'm only happy that she's all better and that she had such a wonderful success last night. That's all the thanks I need."

"You're a good man, Brad. I'm glad my daughter has you in her life."

They stared at each other for a moment, two men joined by love for one woman. But tender moments are often hard for men to share.

Stuart was first to break the silence. "And if you ever leave her, I'll break your neck," he said laughingly.

Brad laughed, too. "No worry on that front."

"Now then," Stuart said, all business again. "What's this fabulous idea you've got?"

Brad began to outline his idea for the series about stagehands. As he spoke, Stuart nodded approvingly. But suddenly Brad felt another searing pain behind his eyes and tried to cover up the wince that automatically came to his face. The now too familiar milky blur crept over his eyes, and he shook his head to clear his vision.

"What's the matter?" asked Stuart.

Brad's vision cleared again. "Oh, nothing," he said as nonchalantly as he could. "Probably too much drink and not enough sleep."

Stuart noticed that Brad's hands trembled slightly. "Are you sure?" he asked.

Brad shrugged. "It's nothing. Really, Stuart. Now, what was I saying?"

As Brad continued to lay out the particulars of his idea, Stuart watched his son-in-law's face, a nagging seed of worry beginning to form in his mind.

Late that afternoon, Brad called Leslie at home.

"Hello!" Her voice sounded so happy she practically sang out the greeting.

"Hello, my darling," Brad said, and felt the intimacy he always did when they spoke on the phone, as if there were no one else on the planet, nothing else, just her voice coming through the cold plastic like a beam of warmth. "I wanted to know if you'd like to go out and celebrate this evening. I can make reservations anywhere you want."

"Oh, no, Brad, come home. I want to spend the whole evening alone, just the two of us, going over every single wonderful word of all the reviews. And then we can watch TV and go to bed."

"How about if we cut out the TV part," Brad murmured.

Leslie smiled and whispered into the phone, "Come home, my love."

After she hung up, she went into the kitchen to prepare supper. She put the roast in the oven, prepared the salad and cleaned the vegetables. Then she laid a beautiful table, with candles, linens, crystal, silver and china. Why some people always saved their wedding presents for special company seemed a mystery to her. Who could be more special than the two of them? She hummed as she went about the work that seemed less like a chore and more an act of love. When she'd finished preparing everything for supper, she went upstairs to change.

By the time Brad got home, Leslie was fresh and glowing from the long, leisurely bath she'd taken. Her hair was loose, falling in rich, thick waves down her back. She wore a rust-colored velvet lounging robe that set off her coloring, brought out the red highlights in her hair and made her skin look even creamier, her eyes more brilliantly dark.

Brad dropped his briefcase on the hall table and moved toward her. In one swift moment, they were in each other's arms, hugging one another as if they hadn't been together for a year.

"You're home," Leslie whispered.

"I'm home," Brad whispered back.

Arm in arm, Leslie led Brad to the living room, where she had lit a fire, not for the cold, but because a fire seemed so cozy. "Would you like a drink?" she asked.

Brad shook his head. "Looking at you and being with you is the only intoxication I need."

They settled onto the couch. Brad kicked his shoes off and wiggled his toes. "Ah . . ."

Leslie giggled. "You sound as if you've been pounding the pavement all day," she said, curling up in the corner of the couch.

"I may not have been on my feet all day, but I've been on my toes," Brad said. "What are you doing sitting way over there?" he asked, drawing her close to him.

As they sat together on the couch, with the dying sun outside and the flames flickering in the fireplace, Brad told her all about his idea for the stories he would do in each of the cities she played. His fingers gently wound long strands of her hair as he spoke, and she nestled near him, happy and content.

"The idea sounds wonderful," Leslie said. "But all your ideas are always good. And this way I'll know for sure that you'll always be by my side. You'll have to go to every city I go to, just to do your stories."

"Leslie," Brad said, kissing the top of her head, "don't you know that I'd travel to the ends of the earth to be with you? My story is the last reason I'd go to a city where you're playing. It's just an idea to give me something to do while you're busy setting up the lights and rehearsing. Something to keep me from feeling like I'm Mr. Leslie Brooks Elliot."

Leslie laughed. "Brad, you know you're anything

but Mr. Leslie Brooks. You're wonderful at your work. No one could ever accuse you of being just an extension of me."

"I guess we're a pretty lucky couple, sweetheart," Brad said.

Leslie was always amazed when she realized how similarly they thought. It often happened in conversations that Brad would say something that reminded her of something she'd recently thought.

"I was thinking that only this morning," Leslie told him. "How lucky I was to have a wonderful career and a wonderful husband. Most people are lucky if they have just one or the other." She snuggled deeper into his arms. "And I've got them both.

"But you know, Brad," she continued, gazing into the fire, "if I ever had to make the choice between my career or you, I'd choose you in a moment."

"What a silly thing to say." Brad hugged her to him. "There's no reason in the world that you'll ever have to make that choice."

It was a conversation he would remember later.

Chapter Two

Falling Leaves

Snapper closed the file marked "Elliot, B.," worry lines furrowing his handsome young brow.

Being a doctor was complicated. When he could help someone, he felt on top of the world. But in cases where a surefire diagnosis was impossible to make, he felt frustrated and helpless. He was particularly dreading this interview with Brad. Brad knew as much medicine as Snapper did, even though Brad hadn't practiced medicine for several years.

He checked his watch. Brad should be arriving any minute. Well, Snapper thought, nervously tamping the file on his desk, there was nothing to do but be direct and plain.

Just then his intercom buzzed, and his nurse's voice filled the room. "Mr. Elliot's here, doctor."

"Thank you, nurse. Please send him in." Snapper took a deep breath, rose from his desk and walked toward the door. He met Brad with his arm outstretched, and they shook hands firmly.

"Sit down, Brad." Snapper indicated the comfortable leather chair he kept near his desk for patients. "I'm not going to ask how you are," he joked, trying

21

to appear relaxed. "After all, I'm supposed to tell you." He sat on the edge of his desk.

"I appreciate your valiant attempt at humor," Brad said, his voice tight. "But spare me your bedside manner. Just hit me with it. There really is something wrong, isn't there?"

Snapper shrugged slightly. "Yes and no. I've run some tests. The tests and the symptoms agree. You've got an inflammation of the optic nerve." He watched Brad's face closely.

Brad nodded, deep in thought. "That makes sense. It would explain the headaches and the . . ." His voice trailed off.

"The problem is that at the moment I don't know the cause," Snapper went on. "So I can only treat you symptomatically. I'm going to put you on cortisone. That will decrease the inflammation, which ought to get rid of the headaches and the spells of temporary . . . blindness."

The word hung heavy in the air.

Brad let out a small laugh, totally devoid of humor. "At least you have the guts to say it. I haven't even let myself think that word."

Snapper tried to keep his voice emotionless and completely professional. "At this point, it's senseless to worry. What we're hoping for is that once we get the inflammation down, whatever caused these symptoms will just go away."

There was a silence in the room as both men finished in their minds what Snapper had not said out loud, that the likelihood of a symptomatic treatment actually curing anything was slight.

"All right," Snapper said briskly, breaking the heavy silence with what he hoped was a professional tone, "I'm sure all this is well known to you, but after all, I am your doctor." He smiled, and this time it was genuine, giving his face a boyish look. "Just humor me while I go through my doctor routine." He deepened his voice and took on the serious air of an older doctor. "You may feel some slight nausea from the cortisone. You may experience an increased appetite. I'm going to give you a shot today, and I want you to come back in ten days for a second. Phone me the minute you feel another headache or blind spell. Any questions?"

Brad smiled, too. The tension he'd been feeling washed away from him for the first time in weeks. Snapper was a good doctor, even if he was young. They would handle this together. "I bet the older ladies love you, Dr. Foster."

Snapper laughed. "My innocent youth and charm sometimes work miracles that medicine can't. Now speaking of ladies, tell Leslie not to worry. If she has any questions, she can call me."

Brad's whole body tensed, and he shook his head. "No. Leslie doesn't know anything about this. I don't want her to."

"You mean you haven't been telling her about your headaches?"

Brad shook his head.

"And you haven't mentioned anything about your temporary blindness?" Snapper sounded incredulous. "But Brad, she's your wife."

Brad looked pained. "Snapper, it took so much to get her back on her feet. Her new season's just begun. I'd do anything to keep her from one second's worth of worry."

"Don't you think you're underestimating Leslie, Brad?" Snapper asked gently.

"Maybe yes, maybe no." Brad looked Snapper in the eye. "But I can't take the chance. I simply can't have her worrying about me. I'm going to continue hiding this from her, and hope that we can cure whatever this is before she even finds out."

Snapper looked worried. "I don't know, Brad. I think you're making a big mistake."

"I disagree with you," Brad said, his voice taking on a hard, determined edge. "And I'm holding you to my decision as my doctor, not my brother-in-law. That means I don't want Stuart or anyone else knowing, because I don't want it to get back to Leslie in any way whatsoever."

"Why don't you think about this? You're making it even harder on yourself, not to mention everyone around you."

"I do not want Leslie to know," Brad said, emphasizing each word. "Is that clear, doctor?"

Snapper's voice sounded strained as he answered, "I'll respect your wishes, Brad, as your doctor. But as your brother-in-law, I'm warning you. You're making a mistake."

Leslie leaned out from the open window of the backseat of the limousine and raised her face to Brad. He bent over and kissed her lightly, his gloved hands covering her long delicate fingers resting on the open window. A slight wind fluttered the end of his plaid scarf and tousled the front lock of his blond hair, which glistened in the last rays of the day. A leaf from the big red maple in their front yard fell on his shoulder, and Leslie reached up to brush it off.

"Darling, are you sure you're warm enough in just your sport coat and scarf?" she asked. "The late afternoons are turning quite cool now."

Brad smiled tenderly. "Of course I am, my sweet. I come from very hearty stock." He tried to keep the irony out of his voice. "Now you have a good trip, practice well, and don't let any handsome admirers buy you dinner and drinks in the hotel."

Leslie picked coquettishly at her black kid gloves and turned her face from his. "If you don't join me soon, who knows what may happen?" She looked up at him teasingly, but the love that suddenly filled her face made his heart contract. His voice grew husky.

"It's just one night that we'll be apart. But it will seem like a year." He leaned down close to her face, and the sweet smell of his breath made her nostrils flare as she breathed him in.

Reaching up, she put her hand on the back of his neck and drew him into a deep kiss. She opened her eyes, wanting to memorize every detail of his face, for even one night apart was too much. But as she opened her eyes, she noticed a deep wince on his face. He seemed to wobble slightly, and he turned his face from hers.

"Brad? What's the matter?"

"Nothing," he said, but his voice seemed to come from far away.

"Brad?" she asked again, beginning to feel frightened.

He blinked, shook his head slightly, and then smiled at her. "It's nothing," he said casually. "Just a little headache." He straightened up.

"All right, Henry," he called to the driver, who had been standing discreetly with his back to them, leaning on the front of the car. "Make sure that Mrs. Elliot gets on the plane, will you?"

"Sure thing," said the driver, hopping in and turning the engine on. The big limousine purred, and the back window slid shut silently. Leslie blew a kiss through the thick glass.

Brad ran his hand along the side of the car as it took

off down the winding street, never taking his eyes from Leslie as she turned and waved to him through the rear window.

He watched as she grew smaller and smaller, his hand raised in a wave. As the big black car disappeared around a curve, a cold wind blew, stinging Brad's eyes with tears.

Leslie hung up the telephone and sank down onto the edge of the big Denver hotel bed. It would seem empty and lonely without Brad.

He had called and made her promise to take a nap before her concert. Something had come up at work that prevented him from coming, he'd said. But he had told her not to worry, that he'd be with her in spirit if not in body, and they'd be together again the very next day. He had reminded her how strong she was now, that together they could do anything. He had said he loved her, and to let his love embrace her as she played, to allow his love to fill her music. And he'd promised never to miss another concert. She had hung up whispering, "Oh, Brad, I love you so."

Brad sat by the phone in their den. It was completely dark outside, and none of the lights were lit in the den. What difference did it make? he asked himself. Blind men don't need lights. Think of how much he'd save on electricity bills, he thought bitterly.

After Leslie's car had left, he'd stood in the driveway and felt his headache grow worse. With it had come the terrifying, lonely darkness that engulfed him longer than it ever had before. He'd stumbled from the driveway and in through the back door, praying none of the neighbors happened to be looking out their windows. He'd stood gasping, holding on to the kitchen cabinet, waiting for his vision to return, waiting for the terrible, throbbing pain in his head to leave him and restore his vision. It had finally passed, leaving him frightened to the bone. This was the first time a bout had lasted for longer than a few seconds.

Later, he'd begun to pack his overnight bag so that he could leave for Denver right from the office the next day. But as he was reaching into the medicine cabinet for his toiletries, another wave had washed over him. In the muddy darkness, his hand had run along the bathroom shelf, knocking bottles into the sink, making him feel helpless and furious. He'd realized he couldn't fly to join Leslie. He couldn't risk her seeing a long attack like these last two.

Now he sat in the dark den, the phone back in its cradle. He felt sick at heart. She had sounded so disappointed. But he had to do it; he had to protect her. He had managed this time, but how many times could he do this before Leslie began to worry?

Brad pounded his fist on the arm of the chair. Why was this happening? Now, when everything in their lives looked so hopeful. . . .

The glowing September sun had faded slowly to a cold, crisp October haze. A hint of the winter to come tickled Genoa City with frosty fingers as the shorter days seemed to fly by.

Leslie got up early each morning and rehearsed. She loved the feeling that came over her each time she sat down at the grand piano in her practice room. Even doing scales was an act of pleasure. Her whole body tingled with the thrill of the lovely music as it moved from her fingers along her arms and filled the whole room.

She felt more productive than she ever had before. Her season was meeting with grand success; reviewers in city after city praised her, and many of her concerts were sold out before she even arrived in the city.

And their lives, hers and Brad's, seemed so normal, somehow. She was busy. He was busy. He had come to all of her concerts. Although difficult to accept at first, she had even gotten used to his not always waiting in the wings. She understood completely when he explained that sometimes he had to be way backstage interviewing the men for his articles. She would've preferred his standing where she could always see him, but Brad was right. He had told her that they were both more mature now, and that she had to view her concerts as work, like any other work. As long as she was strong and healthy, she didn't need the kind of attentive care he'd given her before, during their difficulties. He was right, of course, as he always was.

His articles were a big success, too. Granted, because he was working so hard he sometimes seemed preoccupied. He didn't always come home when he said he would. He was jumpy, sometimes excusing himself from the dinner table even when she was speaking. But after all, Leslie told herself, she couldn't rightfully expect him to become totally subservient to her or to be with her every moment. He had his career, too.

Yes, things were going well. She was happy. Finally, after all they'd been through, they had a normal life.

Brad leaned over Snapper's desk, both hands clenched into fists, the tendons in his neck straining angrily.

"I said increase the cortisone," he said between clenched teeth.

"You're already getting as high a dose as the body can handle," Snapper said warily, not sure how to deal with Brad's anger, even though he knew it wasn't directed at him.

"Don't tell me what I can 'handle,'" Brad burst out, enraged. "I can't keep Leslie from knowing much longer. *That's* what I can't handle. And you'll do as I tell you!" He pointed a finger menacingly at Snapper's face.

"Hey, Brad . . ." Snapper leaned away from Brad. "Calm down, buddy."

It was as if something inside Brad burst, and he sank down in the leather chair, deflated, shaking his head. "I'm sorry, Snapper. I'm really, really sorry. It's just that the strain is unbearable. Lying to Leslie, and she's so trusting." He shook his head. "I can't take it anymore."

Snapper looked at Brad closely, measuring him. "Brad?"

Brad didn't answer.

"Why don't you just tell her?" Snapper asked. "Let her share your burden. She's your wife."

Brad covered his face with his hands. His voice was muffled. "I can't, Snapper. I can't. I know what will happen. She'll start cancelling tours, calling off concerts, just to be with me. Everything she's worked for will go down the drain. I just can't do it. I love her too much." Suddenly he glanced up with such a pleading look on his face that Snapper was almost ashamed to see a man as strong as Brad looking like that. "Snapper, please? Let's just try to increase the dosage. It's not addictive, you know that. There's already something wrong with me, anyway. A little experimental medicine can't do too much harm. Besides, it's my body. I'll take the risk. I'll even sign a paper saying I insisted that you increase the dosage."

Snapper sighed. "All right, Brad. Roll up your sleeve."

Leslie clipped on her diamond earrings and made the final touches to her hair. There was a knock at her dressing room door, and the stage manager stuck his head in the door.

"Telegrams, Mrs. Elliot."

She was used to getting telegrams from fans who sent her well-wishes before each concert. Sometimes they even made requests for certain pieces, as if her whole program weren't planned in advance. It had been Brad's idea to wait until after the concert to open them. That way she didn't get ruffled by conflicting emotions; she always felt as if she were letting her fans down if she didn't honor their requests.

"Thank you, Bill." Leslie accepted the telegrams and tossed them onto her dressing table. "How much time do I have?"

"You go on in five minutes."

"I can't imagine what's happened to my husband. I wonder if his plane's been delayed."

"It's possible. It's a nasty night out there."

"Well, I'm sure he'll be here when he can." Leslie smiled, thinking of Brad. "He's never let me down yet."

After the concert, she began to be concerned. Brad was nowhere in sight. The stage manager told her that he hadn't seen Brad, but no accidents had been reported at the airport, so she shouldn't worry.

Listlessly she skimmed through the telegrams from well-wishers, but she sat upright when she saw one signed "Brad."

Darling stop Nothing serious stop My mother not feeling well stop Repeat do not worry stop See you at home stop Sure your concert was grand success stop I love you and will never stop

Leslie glanced at her watch. It was almost midnight here in San Francisco; what time was it in Chicago? Should she call Brad's mother to find out how she was? Or would she wake her? Maybe it would be better to wait until morning, Leslie thought sensibly.

But by the time she'd changed her clothes and was driven back to the hotel, she began to worry. It must be very serious for Brad to have flown to Chicago to see his mother. She'd better call.

Mrs. Elliot's sleepy voice answered the phone.

"Mother Elliot? It's Leslie," she said, embarrassed to have awakened her.

"Leslie, how wonderful to hear from you. But my gracious, what time is it?" Her voice still sounded sleepy and confused. Suddenly she became alarmed. "Is everything all right, dear? Why are you calling?"

Stunned, Leslie stammered for a moment. "Oh, I—I was just calling you to see how you were. . . ." She hoped Mrs. Elliot would fill her in.

Mrs. Elliot sounded surprised. "Of course I'm all right. Unless you know something I don't." She chuckled.

"No, no, of course not. Well, I'm sorry to have bothered you." Leslie paused. How could she say this delicately? "I suppose as long as I've gotten your household up, you might as well put my husband on the phone."

It was Mrs. Elliot's turn to be confused. "Oh, my, Leslie," she said nervously. "What makes you think Brad's here?"

Again Leslie stammered, shame beginning to wash over her. Her husband had lied. There could only be one reason. She tried to laugh. "Oh, I . . . I must've gotten my days confused. You know, with both of us on the road so much, sometimes we forget where the other one is." It sounded lame even to her ears.

Mrs. Elliot still sounded nervous on the other end. "Yes, yes, I'm sure that happens the way you two travel."

There was another awkward silence.

"Well," Leslie and Mrs. Elliot began at the same time, then they both laughed nervously. Leslie began again:

"Well, I'm sorry to have disturbed you. It's just life in the fast lane." She tried to laugh.

"Good night, dear." Mrs. Elliot couldn't hide the concern in her voice.

"Good night, Mother Elliot. Sleep well," Leslie said, and slowly hung up the phone.

Leslie quietly let herself in the front door, set her bag down softly in the hall and stood listening for Brad. There were no sounds in the house. Just one night before their beautiful big home had been a haven to her; now it seemed empty and cold.

She hung her fur in the hall closet and continued to tell herself what she had told herself all last night and during the long plane ride back to Genoa City. There was a normal, reasonable explanation. But the more she thought the words, the hollower they seemed.

Because now little pieces of the puzzle were fitting together to form a picture that was becoming terrifyingly clear. His scarcity. His somehow never being exactly where he said he was going to be. His suddenly turning from her with a pained look on his face. His excusing himself from the dinner table. His turning his face away from her. Turning away from her. Turning away from her. *He was turning away from her.*

The words echoed in her mind. He no longer loved her. He loved someone else. And whoever the some-one else was, she was taking Brad away.

Whatever she did, she would not allow herself to cry. She went into the living room and sat regally in the cool green silk-covered chair, her back straight, her hands folded neatly in her lap and her legs crossed primly at the ankles. The only telltale sign of the passion that raged within her was one foot, which wiggled slightly as she waited for Brad to come home.

Brad sat on the edge of the couch, his head in his hands. Leslie remained in the same chair she had been sitting in for the last two hours.

"Leslie, Leslie, Leslie," was all Brad could say as he shook his head wearily. He looked up at her, his eyes pleading. "But darling, why did you call my mother?"

Leslie held herself in check. The only sign of her anger was a sudden darkening of her pupils and two red spots high on her pale white cheeks. "The question, one would think," she said icily, "is not *why* a wife would call her mother-in-law, since the wife had received a telegram saying her mother-in-law was ill enough to keep her husband from joining her. The question is, rather, why a husband would lie to his wife."

There was a terrible black silence in the room, filled with unspoken accusations, unanswered questions, longing and tears.

Brad's mind raced over conversations. Snapper warning him, telling him to confide in Leslie. He opened his mouth, on the verge of telling Leslie everything. Even risking another possible breakdown would be worth banishing the betrayal and suspicion he saw in her deep eyes. But then a second conversation went through his mind—one they had had in this very room: when Leslie had said half-jokingly that she'd give up her career in a minute if it were a choice between that and Brad.

He couldn't do that to her, not after she'd worked so hard. If he really loved her, he'd never take music away from her. Never.

Leslie watched Brad's face. She watched the pain that was clear in his beloved features, beloved even now, even thinking he'd betrayed her. But for her own sake, she couldn't show him anything she felt. She would hold on, even if she had to bite her lip to keep from crying out, "Brad, Brad, don't leave me! No one can love you more than I!" No, she'd remain silent.

She saw him reach a decision and, suddenly fearful, braced herself. Her knuckles turned white as her hands gripped the mahogany arms of her chair. She watched him, almost through a haze, as if none of it were real, as her husband, her beloved husband, stood and walked toward her, a pleading look in his eyes.

Oh, Lord, she prayed silently, please make me strong enough to bear the words when he says he loves another.

Brad came toward her and knelt before her chair. He looked up at her for a moment, then asked in a very quiet voice, "Leslie, do you love me?"

She wouldn't answer. She couldn't trust herself not

to break down and weep, not to throw herself at him and beg him to give up this other woman. She had to hold on and be strong.

She stared at him stonily.

He looked down at his feet, then back up to her. "Leslie, do you trust me?"

It was all she could do to hold on. "Why should I trust a man who lies to me to cover a dirty affair?" She spat out the words, knifelike icicles slashing the air.

The look on his face was utterly surprised, innocent astonishment. "An affair?" he asked incredulously. "Oh, Leslie, Leslie." He shook his head, almost laughing in spite of himself. "Leslie, my love, my wife, my darling, that you could ever think that I could even *look* at another woman, let alone have an *affair.*"

Leslie was confused. Her hand, unwillingly, like a small bird, flew to her heart. It was all she could do to keep from weeping. She wanted to believe him. His innocence seemed so genuine. She didn't think he could perform so well or lie to her like that.

"Darling," Brad said, looking her in the eye, "I love you more than my own life."

His words hung in the room, echoing between them.

"But then where were you?" Leslie's voice sounded small and frightened.

Brad tried to take her hand, but she pulled it back. Very seriously, he said, "If you love me"—he looked up at her to see small stinging tears forming in her eyes—"which I know you do, you'll trust me."

"How can I trust you, Brad?" Her voice wavered. "You lied to me."

Brad stood and walked across the room, his head

bowed. He would've given anything to unburden himself to her, to have her share his fright, and most of all to regain her trust. But he couldn't. Not if he loved her.

He turned and said from across the room, "Leslie, I've never asked anything like this of you before. But now I'm asking you for something that until now you've given whole-heartedly. I'm asking for your trust. I lied last night for a reason. A good reason, but a reason, my love, that I cannot tell you. Believe me, though, my love, my dearest, please believe me, I never will, never *can*, love another woman. This has absolutely nothing to do with another woman."

Leslie wanted to throw herself into his arms. She wanted all of this to have never happened. She wanted him to tell her the real reason—*whatever* it was—so that she would no longer feel this horrible, remaining suspicion. But she couldn't throw herself into his arms. Instead, she sat in her chair, across the room from him.

"I will accept you saying you're not having an affair, Brad. But I see no earthly reason why you should ever have to lie to me."

Brad wanted to throw himself at her feet, to enfold her in his arms, to tell her everything. But he couldn't. Instead, he leaned against the credenza, across the room from her.

"Please trust me, my love. Please."

And so each remained, prisoners of pride, each wanting the other more than anything in the world, each separated by the distance of a room—and the infinite universe of a lie.

Chapter Three

Darkening Days

Moonlight fell across their bed. Brad's breathing was even and smooth. Leslie lay on her side, staring at her sleeping husband.

Her eyes traveled over his thick, straight hair, tousled by sleep, the blond strands almost white in the moonlight. Her glance continued along his smooth forehead, his patrician eyebrows, and down along his straight, handsome nose. His mouth was slack in sleep, but even so, it was a strong, manly mouth, as was his jaw. Her eyes caressed the beautiful, well-defined muscles of his neck.

Over the past weeks he had been so attentive. He had listened to her play. He had complimented her. He had brought her silly gifts, like a teddy bear, and lovely ones, like the gold piano charm that hung now from the bracelet around her wrist.

She lifted her hand, and the tiny piano glittered in the moonlight. Tears stung her eyes. Wasn't this an old story? she asked herself. A husband strays and then, in a fit of guilt and remorse, showers his wife with gifts and attention?

She glanced back at Brad. He lay sleeping so

innocently. For the thousandth time since that awful evening in the living room, she saw again the astonished innocence in his face when she accused him of having an affair. That couldn't possibly have been an act. Could it?

Oh, Brad, she pleaded in her mind, give me some sign, something that will tell me what's wrong.

Brad moved in his sleep. Suddenly his peaceful, sleeping face contorted in a grimace of pain. His head tossed back and forth on the pillow, and he groaned.

Instinctively, Leslie reached out to him and gathered him into her arms as she would a child. "Shhh," she whispered in his ear. "It's just a nightmare, Brad, it's all right."

"Leslie, Leslie," he mumbled, his voice tortured.

"Yes, my love. I'm here," she crooned, stroking his hair.

He nestled his head on her shoulder, and whatever he'd been dreaming seemed to fade away.

Why couldn't he trust her with whatever was troubling him? How could she be a real wife to him if he felt he had to protect her from the realities of life? What could possibly be so horrible that she couldn't know? Was he having financial trouble? But that was ridiculous. They could live lavishly on the money she made. And even if she never earned another penny, there was always her father. No, it couldn't be money. Was someone ill? But she could handle that, she could face whatever it was, if only he would tell her. The only truth that she felt she couldn't face was his loving another. But he had seemed so innocent of that. Hadn't he?

Leslie continued to stroke Brad's head as one unanswered question followed the next, like a snake with its tail in its mouth, in a deepening spiral, until she, too, fell into a troubled sleep.

Brad let the steaming hot water pound down on his shoulders, fighting the stabbing pains that he knew were the precursor to the black that would engulf him. He heard Leslie knock at the bathroom door, and as the blackness overtook him completely, he heard her say, "Brad? Can I come in?"

The bathroom door opened, but the sound came as from a great distance as the pain raged inside his head. He heard Leslie's voice as she warbled happily, "Darling, my itinerary just arrived, and it's fabulous!"

Silently he prayed that the frosted glass of the stall shower and the steam in the bathroom would be enough to prevent her from seeing him holding on to the wall for dear life. He listened as Leslie prattled on about the East Coast leg of her tour. How excited she was that she'd be playing Boston's great Philharmonic Hall. What an honor it was that they'd booked her in Carnegie Hall—and had even scheduled her to play in the Kennedy Center in Washington. He heard the happiness in her voice and was grateful that she didn't seem to notice he wasn't answering.

Laughingly she chided, "Brad, you've been in the shower so long! Don't use up all the hot water, darling." And then he heard the bathroom door close.

He leaned against the wall, with the steam all around him, the water pounding down on him. His hands slid along the slippery wall of the shower, and he gritted his teeth and raised his head up, up toward heaven, pleading to be freed from this nightmare.

* * *

THE YOUNG AND THE RESTLESS

The Boston tour was a smash success. Every night for two weeks, Leslie played to packed houses. Every day, she and Brad explored the city. They visited Fisherman's Wharf, The Commons and Beacon Hill. They giggled like children, playing with a Boston accent, saying, "Pahk the cah in Hahvahd Yahd." They ate Boston baked beans and clam chowder. Brad stood by smiling while Leslie frittered away an afternoon in Filene's basement.

But at certain moments each had trouble meeting the other's eye, as if the hilarity were slightly forced, the giddiness brittle. By unspoken consent they said nothing, even when they found themselves in each other's arms, clinging to one another with an unnamed, unspoken fear.

Brad was getting rather good at hiding his attacks, but he also knew that most of them came by chance at times when he could cover them up. He lived in dread of the moment when it would be impossible to hide.

The moment came in New York, high atop the Empire State Building. They had been kissing and laughing in the wind that whipped around them. Brad slipped a coin into one of the telescopes, and Leslie peered through it. "Oh, look"—she pointed —"there's Radio City, and there's the Chrysler Building."

Suddenly Brad felt the onslaught of an attack and knew he had to think fast. There was nothing to hold on to up here. Leslie would soon tire of the telescope and want to move on. Then he thought of an idea.

"Let's play a game, Leslie," he said, trying to keep his voice light even though his vision was fading quickly. "Let's pretend that I can't see. You have to describe everything to me, everything you see, and then you have to take me back to the elevator."

Leslie looked at him, startled. "What a horrible game," she said, searching his face.

He smiled, trying to keep his expression normal, hoping that he was looking at her.

"No, it's not. It'll be fun." He closed his eyes. "All right, my love. I'm totally in your hands." He reached out toward her and, groping, found her shoulder.

"I don't know, Brad," Leslie said uncertainly.

"Please, Leslie, play this game with me," he pleaded, gripping her shoulder tightly and hoping his smile looked natural.

He felt her shrug. "It seems silly to me, but if you insist." She began describing what she saw.

"That's wonderful," Brad said. "Now take me to the elevator. And remember, I can't see anything. My eyes are closed."

He could hear the slight exasperation in her voice as she said, "Now take three steps. That's it."

He heard the elevator doors open. She directed him into it, saying nervously to the elevator operator, "We're just playing a silly game." She led him into the back of the elevator, and he leaned his head against the wall.

By the time the elevator reached ground level, his vision had returned. He opened his eyes and led her out, laughing and saying what a good seeing-eye dog she would make.

But in the long, dark ride down in the elevator, he had made a decision.

Leslie stared out of the window of the Metroliner as it raced through a particularly bleak section of Pennsylvania. Oil refineries dotted the flat landscape, and the Delaware River tried to hold up its graceful head as it flowed through what had once been a bounteous valley but was now sullied with the refuse of industry.

"Yes, but Brad," Leslie finally said, turning to face him and continuing the conversation she'd been having in her mind. "Washington just won't be as much fun with Laurie as it would be with you."

Brad turned a page of the *New York Times,* trying to make light of the conversation. "I know, dear," he said as he scanned the page. "But I told you, a big story came up at the newspaper that they thought only I could handle properly. I'll be with you for the beginning of your tour, and at the end. Laurie will join you just so that you're not alone for ten days. You're making more of it than there is." He flicked his newspaper. "Don't you have something to read?"

Leslie was stung. Brad seemed so cold. She turned her face away from him again, leaned her forehead against the cool glass of the window and watched as the cold, gray landscape sped by.

Chicago. The Windy City. And windy it was, as Brad paid the taxi driver, picked up his suitcase from the curb and stood for a moment looking up at Chicago General, the city's largest hospital. The hospital where he had once worked.

He bent his head, holding onto his hat with one hand. When the wind whipped his raincoat open, he grabbed it closed and made his way up the familiar, grand marble steps of the main entrance.

But the wind outside was nothing compared with the wind inside him as he made his way toward admissions.

All around him the halls seemed to echo faraway voices, as if he could still hear the metallic, impatient sound of the paging system. "Dr. Elliot, wanted in

O.R. four." "Dr. Elliot, please pick up the emergency phone."

Brad went through admissions as if in a fog, answering what seemed like unending questions. How strange it felt to be on the patient side of a medical procedure.

He had his blood taken and his blood pressure checked. He allowed a young intern to knock at his knees and listen to his heart, all the while wondering if this young man could hear in his stethoscope the thoughts racing through his mind.

Could the intern see the operating room? See the little boy, so tiny and helpless under the full glare of the operating lights? Could the intern tell that Brad's heart began pounding as he stood over the little body, while the nurse spoke quickly: "Blood pressure falling. Breathing labored. Heart not responding." Could the intern see all the tiny arteries as Brad sweated, trying to stop the little boy's bleeding? As Brad carefully, precisely clamped shut as many arteries as he could? As the nurse's dreaded voice kept repeating, coldly, clinically, "Blood pressure falling. Blood pressure falling. Doctor, blood pressure falling dangerously."

"Mr. Elliot?" The intern's voice came as if from far away. "Mr. Elliot, are you all right?"

"Of course I'm not," Brad snapped. "Why do you think I'm checking into the hospital, idiot?"

The young intern looked crestfallen.

Brad was stricken. "I'm sorry. I didn't mean to snap at you. I'm just edgy."

The intern smiled sympathetically. "That's all right, sir. Most people are nervous when I talk to them."

Memories continued to haunt Brad as the intern

guided him down long, polished halls toward the new wing.

How could he have known that the little boy was his own son? But would it have mattered if he had known? Of course it would've. If he'd only known it was his son, he would've had another doctor perform the surgery. The boy might be alive today. Why hadn't Barbara told him that it was their son? Barbara, Barbara . . .

Through the haze of his memories, he saw a nurse at the far end of the hall. It was his mind playing tricks on him, he told himself. The thick blond hair curling out from under the nurse's cap. The voluptuous body that no starched uniform could hide. The sensuous walk, even when she moved in the quick, efficient way of a nurse.

As the nurse drew closer, her brisk steps slowed.

"Brad?" He heard a voice from what seemed another life.

"Barbara?" He stopped in his tracks.

They stared at one another with all the mingled shock, nervousness and pleasure of two people who had once loved deeply.

"What are you doing here?" she asked, finding her voice first.

"I've come for some tests." He shrugged. "It's nothing serious."

The intern felt as if he were intruding. "Miss Randall, I wonder if you have time to take Mr. Elliot to his room?" he asked, handing her Brad's chart.

"Excuse me?" she said, not having heard the intern's words over the pounding of her heart. When she realized what he'd asked her, she took the chart and said in her most professional voice, "Of course. Mr. Elliot, will you come this way?"

They continued walking in silence, each wanting to

ask a tho⁀⁀nd questions, neither knowing where to begin.

Brad quietly closed the door of the doctor's office and leaned against the wall. He was grateful that the doctor was a relative newcomer to Chicago General —at least since Brad's time. Not having a personal relationship made it easier to bear. Almost.

Again, he saw the doctor's professionally sympathetic face. And heard the words. *Incurable. Progressive, incurable blindness.*

His first thoughts had been for Leslie. Leslie, his beloved. He couldn't expect her to lead a blind man around for the rest of her life. And he knew with dreadful certainty that if she knew, she would insist on giving up her career, carting him from one specialist to another, giving up her life for his. He couldn't do it to the woman he loved.

He had to think. He had to stall for time. He had to figure something out. He had to protect his love.

Laurie was peeved. The last thing she wanted to do was stop working on her book to go to Washington to baby-sit for Leslie. Precious Leslie. Leslie, who always had to have her hand held. Leslie, whose career was always the most important. Leslie this and Leslie that. It made Laurie sick.

And Brad had been so disgustingly sweet over the phone. He was always sweet to her when he wanted something—for precious Leslie. Flattering her, saying that she may be younger, but she was so much more sophisticated than Leslie and that he was relying on Laurie to look out for her sister in the big city. Saying he hated to bother her, but he had a story to do in Chicago and didn't want Leslie to be all alone in Washington.

Laurie reached for the phone. When she heard Stuart's clipped voice on the other end, she smiled sweetly and told him that she was going to Washington to be with Leslie.

"It must be a really important scoop you're sending Brad off to do in Chicago. Don't you have any other ace reporters over there?"

As she listened to Stuart's response, she curled the telephone wire around her finger and raised her eyebrows. "Oh, really?" she cooed into the phone. "No, no, I'm *sure* I must've misunderstood him."

As soon as she'd rung off, she began packing. This trip was beginning to look more interesting.

Brad sat in an armchair in the patients' solarium, a large glass-enclosed room that looked out on the lake. He refused to wear pajamas, but he had allowed himself to exchange his usual jacket, starched shirt and trousers for comfortable slacks and a sweater.

The cold gray Chicago day did little to warm his heart. Barbara had dropped by his room in the morning and suggested that they meet during her lunch break. It was fine with him; he felt no guilt about seeing her. Their first few times together had been awkward, but he realized that his love for Leslie was strong and true. What had been between Barbara and him had been good, but it was long over and had never had the depth of his love for Leslie.

Barbara had told him about her new love, a man who sounded much more suited to her. Over the past week, their relationship had settled into the comfort of good, close old friends. In fact, he was grateful she was there. It made the going a little less rough.

He felt a warm hand on his shoulder and heard her deep voice. "Hey, killer. How's it going?"

He reached out and squeezed her hand, drawing her in front of him.

"Here, let me look at you. I don't know how many more times I'll be able to."

She settled herself on the window ledge in front of him, resting her hands on her knees, and looked him in the eye with fondness. "Now, my friend, no feeling sorry for yourself. You have some planning to do." Her voice became businesslike. "You have to see the therapist, who will begin instructing you about how to haul your carcass around without eyes. Then you have to get in touch with these people." She handed him a business card. "They have the best seeing-eye dogs in the city. And you have to start learning Braille. It'll be easier while you still have your sight."

Brad looked away. "The length of the spells is increasing," he said, his voice tight. "I spent a good hour this morning smashing around my room like Frankenstein." He let out a humorless laugh.

He could hear the tenderness in Barbara's voice. "I know, killer. It isn't easy. You're doing great. You're a real champ. Now . . . when is Leslie's tour over?"

"Leslie?!" Brad sounded shocked.

"Yes, Leslie. Your wife. Remember her?" Barbara said, trying to make a joke of it.

Brad simply stared at her.

"Brad," Barbara said gently, "this entire grueling process of rehabilitation will be that much easier as soon as Leslie can get here."

Brad's eyes widened.

"You see," she went on, ignoring his expression, "a wife has a lot to learn, too. You're not the only one who has some readjustments to make. If the two of you learn together, while you still have your vision, the road will be much smoother later on."

"No, no, no, Barbara," Brad said, determination in his voice. "I'm not telling Leslie anything about this."

"Are you crazy? How can you not tell your wife you're going blind?"

Brad said nothing. He turned his head from Barbara and stared out the far window.

"Brad, look at me."

He continued staring out the window.

"All right, then. Just listen to me." Her voice softened. "Brad, didn't you learn anything from what happened between us?"

He stared, remaining silent.

Barbara sighed. "I always thought you were smart. I guess I was wrong. Well, if you didn't learn anything, at least I did." Her voice took on a thoughtful tone. "I learned that if you love someone, really love them, then you don't hide anything from them. That's what love is all about. And if you *do* hide something big, you end up losing the one you love."

She saw the muscles in Brad's neck tighten and noticed the way he swallowed painfully, as if there were a lump in his throat. But still he sat silent, staring away from her . . . his mind made up, but his heart breaking.

Laurie sat in an armchair in Leslie's dressing room, swinging her crossed leg and letting out long puffs from a cigarette. She picked up one of the telegrams idly and read aloud in a mocking voice, "Looking forward to hearing Chopin. Thank you in advance. Signed, a sincere fan." She rolled her eyes. "How truly touching," she said, tossing the telegram down and puffing at her cigarette.

Leslie wished Laurie wouldn't insist on being in her dressing room before each concert. It made her jittery. She wished she wouldn't read her telegrams, but she didn't say anything. After all, it was nice of Laurie to drop everything and be with her while Brad was away. How she missed his reassuring presence.

"I wonder how Brad's doing?"

Laurie's voice startled her, as if her sister had been reading her mind. She began applying her mascara. "He sounded fine last night when he called. I'm sure he's as busy as a beaver working on his story." She dabbed at the excess mascara with a tissue and began on the other eye.

"You know, it's funny," Laurie said.

Leslie only half listened, intent on getting her mascara applied correctly.

"But when I spoke to Daddy," Laurie continued smoothly, "he didn't know what story Brad was working on in Chicago."

Leslie stopped dabbing and looked at her sister in the mirror. Laurie smiled sweetly at her through the mirror and took a big puff on her cigarette.

"Well, it must be some secret story they don't want anyone to know about," Leslie snapped, dabbing away furiously. A big blob of mascara dropped under her eye, and as she reached for the cold cream and another tissue, she said between clenched teeth, "You know, Laurie, I really wish you wouldn't sit here and chitchat while I'm dressing for a performance."

Laurie simply smiled at her sister in the dressing room mirror, the bright lights throwing a harsh glare across her red lips.

Next morning, the reviews noted that although Mrs. Brooks-Elliot usually played flawlessly and with great feeling, there had been one false note struck during a particularly sweet movement of Mozart.

Chapter Four

Winter Deepens

The silence in the dining room was broken only by the sound of silverware on china. Finally Leslie could stand it no longer. "How was work today?" she asked, the words impersonal, like polite conversation between strangers assigned the same dining table on a train.

"Good! Fine!" Brad knew he sounded far too hearty. But how could he say he'd spent most of the day pretending he was doing research in the newspaper library, while actually waiting out long, unending hours of darkness?

"I spoke to Daddy today." Leslie tried to keep the accusation out of her voice. "He mentioned that you haven't been at your desk much lately."

"That's because I've been in the library, researching something," Brad burst out in spite of himself. "Ask the librarian. She'll tell you."

Coolly, Leslie cut a piece of meat. "I have no intention of checking up on my husband's whereabouts, Brad. It's demeaning."

They continued eating in silence.

"I don't suppose"—Leslie's cool voice cut through

the silence like a knife—"that your 'busy' library schedule will allow you much time to help with the preparations for the benefit concert?"

Brad put down his knife and fork and leaned across the table toward his wife. "Leslie, Leslie, what's happening between us?"

"Nothing is happening between us, Brad." Leslie enunciated each word clearly and coldly. "Absolutely nothing."

"Leslie, I can't go on like this," Brad pleaded.

Leslie felt hope spring up in her heart. She loved him so much—maintaining this distance and coldness was becoming impossible. She wanted nothing more than to be close again. She leaned toward him and for the first time in weeks allowed the love she felt for him to show in her face and voice. Her whole body strained toward him. "Then tell me, Brad. Tell me whatever this awful, awful secret is that you're trying to hide. I can take it, Brad, I promise. Just tell me what it is." She felt tears begin.

"Leslie . . ." Brad reached his hand toward her across the table. "Please trust me, I beg of you. I'm acting out of love for you. I promise on everything I hold dear, my silence is an act of love."

Leslie threw her napkin onto the table and stood up. "Don't speak to me of love!" For the first time ever she raised her voice to him. "You don't know the meaning of the word. You think that love is holding hands and never sharing any problems? You're wrong, Brad. You don't love me. If you loved me, you would tell me what's going on in your life, and not leave me alone, shut out, suspecting the worst."

She waited for Brad to say something, anything. But he remained silent, his hand lying lifeless, stretching toward her, a look of pain crossing his face.

"Say something, Brad!" she pleaded. "You're losing me!"

But he merely lowered his head.

Leslie ran out of the room.

Brad wanted desperately to follow, but he didn't. He sat at the dining room table, hearing the sobs of the woman he loved filter down the stairs from their bedroom to pierce his black prison.

The intrusive sound of the phone ringing irritated Laurie. Quickly she finished the sentence she was working on and snatched up the receiver. "Hello!" she snapped, her voice impatient. For a moment, all she heard were the pinging sounds of a long-distance connection, and then a woman's voice came on the line.

"Is this Laurie Brooks?"

"Yes."

There was a hesitation, then the woman went on, "Excuse me for disturbing you. I'm Barbara Randall, an old friend of Brad Elliot's."

"Oh?" said Laurie, her voice growing smoother as interest replaced irritation.

"I hope I'm not taking any liberties I shouldn't be. . . ." The woman hesitated.

"I'm sure you're not." Laurie's voice was reassuring.

"The reason I'm calling is . . ." She hesitated once more, then plunged on, "I felt it was important that someone in his family know. I racked my brain, and finally decided that if I told you, Leslie's sister, I wouldn't really be breaking any confidences. But I just can't sleep at night, thinking no one knows."

Laurie reached for a cigarette. She listened and nodded encouragingly as Barbara went on talking.

Smoke curled around her, and her eyes narrowed to slits as she took in every word. "You were absolutely right to call me," she purred at the end of the conversation. "You can leave it all in my hands."

Lance Prentiss leaned casually against a giant marble column, his hands jammed into the pockets of his tuxedo trousers as easily as if they were tennis togs. His broad, athletic shoulders strained against the well-cut tux, and his golden hair shone in sharp contrast to his deeply tanned face. Laconically, he surveyed the scene beneath him.

Wide marble stairs led from where he stood in the large entrance hall into a broad reception room. A file of people slowly snaked its way past the receiving line and flowed through several giant archways into the vast ballroom itself. He supposed all the white-veined marble, gilt and mirrors were splendid enough—for a place in what he considered the sticks.

As one of America's wealthiest industrialists, he sometimes had to give up a more interesting party of artists or showgirls to attend a tiresome benefit performance. He wasn't even sure what this one was for: cancer, whales, starving children, who knew? But his mother had checked it off in her spindly handwriting on the list of events he absolutely *had* to attend this month.

Dutifully he'd gone to the concert, expecting to be bored, as he usually was at these bumpkin affairs. But the pianist had piqued his interest. Her playing had been genuinely lyrical . . . and so had her looks. At least looking for her would give him something to do during what seemed like an otherwise boring evening.

He felt a cool, slender hand slip underneath his

arm. "Ah, Contessa." He smiled, his teeth white against his tan. "Back from powdering your nose so soon?"

The contessa's Roman nose was as long as her family tree. Too bad she didn't have a nickel, Lance thought. But they suited one another. Her title, his money. He just hoped this bunch didn't curtsy when he introduced her like those clowns in Akron or Dacron or wherever he'd taken her the last time.

"Gather up your tiara and title, my dear, and let's go wow 'em."

The contessa smiled. She could put up with his biting sense of humor forever, if he would only marry her and give her American citizenship and cash.

They glided gracefully down the marble steps, arm in arm. The contessa felt Lance's body perk up, and she followed his glance to the last woman in the receiving line: the slender, delicate beauty with chestnut hair. It was the pianist. In a simple long black dress and a single strand of pearls, she was exquisite. Suddenly the contessa wanted to ring the neck of the little designer who had convinced her that this shocking-pink monstrosity with the giant tulle bow sticking up a foot higher than her head on one shoulder would do wonders for setting off the other shoulder, which now felt bony and naked.

They moved through the line. A good-looking self-possessed young woman in a turquoise sequined strapless gown sized them up and introduced herself as Laurie Brooks, her mother's daughter. The contessa wondered if that were an American idiom she hadn't learned. Laurie handed them down the line, smiling at Lance a bit longer than was necessary. Mrs. Brooks, elegant in silver lamé, murmured politely. Mr. Brooks pumped the contessa's hand heartily, saying what an honor it was to have her there. Out of the corner of her eye, she noticed that Lance was already shaking hands with the pianist.

Lance bowed and looked Leslie directly in the eye. "I can't tell you how much I enjoyed your performance tonight."

"Thank you," she said politely, her eyes already starting to move down the line.

But he held on to her hand. "I'm serious," he said.

"I'm serious, too, when I say thank you," she said, nodding her head graciously and withdrawing her hand. Her voice was cool and rich. She turned to the man who had just joined her at the end of the reception line. "Ah, Brad, I was just beginning to wonder where you were."

She said it evenly enough, but Lance detected a slight edge to her voice and looked with interest at the man, whom he assumed was her husband.

"Brad," said Leslie, "this is . . . I'm sorry, what did you say your name was?"

"Lance." He looked her in the eye. "Lance Prentiss."

Brad reached out, and they shook hands.

"Is it too obvious," Lance said, "to say what a lucky man you are to have such a beautiful *and* talented wife?"

Brad smiled politely and put his hand possessively on Leslie's shoulder. Leslie turned to shake hands with the contessa, and the reception line moved on.

Champagne flowed, aided by waiters who moved effortlessly through the ballroom, balancing huge silver trays kept continuously full. The Peter Duchin Band played on, alternating waltzes with slow, big-band sounds. Laughter filled the ballroom as groups shifted and changed, having lost the initial formality of the reception line. The ball was in full swing.

Lance left the contessa with a short, fat, bald man with diamond dollar-bill-sign studs in his tux. Grabbing two glasses of champagne off a passing tray, he made his way through the crowd toward Leslie, who stood elegantly surrounded by a group of laughing people.

"Madam." He bowed formally, offering her a glass.

She shook her head laughingly and made a gesture of refusal with her hands. Lance noticed what beautiful long fingers she had. "No, thank you," she said, smiling. "I've had quite enough for one evening." Her smile was very broad. "Two glasses is my limit."

"But champagne is an elixir," he said, urging the glass on her. "You look so much freer, younger, and if possible, even more beautiful."

She continued to refuse the drink, but without her knowing how, Lance had managed to maneuver her away from the group of people she'd been standing with. They stood facing one another, the party flowing around them.

Brad paused at the top of the stairs. He could see beyond the reception room and through the giant archways into the ballroom. At the far end was the bandstand. Couples whirled gracefully; clusters of people stood or sat at the tables around the edges of the vast room. But to Brad, all of it was a dim, miasmic swirl of colors and light. He saw only one thing with clarity, an image reflected forever back and forth between the giant mirrors that lined the room: Leslie standing with the tall blond man who'd shown such obvious interest in her in the receiving line.

It was better this way, Brad thought. At least he wouldn't have to worry about her. He glanced once around the room, picking out people in the crowd. He saw Stuart's shining hair and straight back: his father-in-law, who'd been so good to him. He saw a flash of silver fabric: his mother-in-law, who'd always been the picture of grace. All the people he'd known now for several years, all standing chatting easily with one another. He bade them farewell in his mind and turned his eyes back to Leslie.

Oh, Leslie, Leslie, he thought, staring at her, please forgive me for what I'm about to do. I do it out of love for you.

He turned swiftly, went to the cloakroom and gave the hat-check girl a note. "Please see that Mrs. Elliot gets this note in an hour. It's very important." His head began pounding.

"Are you all right, Mr. Elliot?" asked the girl.

"No, as a matter of fact." Brad tried to seem nonchalant. "I have a terrible headache. But if Mrs. Elliot knows I'm leaving, she'll want to come with me. That's why it's so important that she get my note in an hour. Can I rely on you?" he asked, handing her five dollars.

"You don't have to do that, Mr. Elliot," she protested, pushing the money back toward him. "Just go home and take some aspirin."

"Good-bye," Brad said, leaving the tip and thinking how sad it was that the only person he was saying good-bye to was a kindly hatcheck girl. He went out through the grand doors.

Laurie came out of the ladies' room freshly combed and perfumed and intent on seeing if she couldn't "accidentally" bump into that good-looking blond man who had arrived with the foreign scarecrow on his arm. She took a few steps but stopped when she saw Brad at the top of the stairs, staring down into the ballroom. She watched as he stood there, watched as he seemed to make up his mind about something and straighten his shoulders, watched as he strode toward the checkroom, watched him hand the note to the girl, watched his hand go up to his forehead, watched him take his coat and leave.

She walked across the marble floor, her high heels clacking, and said easily to the girl, "Is Mr. Elliot ill?"

"Why, yes, he said he had a headache. But he doesn't want Mrs. Elliot to know he's leaving because he's afraid she'll want to leave early with him. You won't tell her, will you?"

Laurie graced the girl with a reassuring smile. "Of course not." She fumbled in her bag and handed the girl her check number and ten dollars. "We'll just keep this between ourselves. But I'll follow him and make sure he's all right. Remember now," she called over her shoulder as she threw her coat around her and left hurriedly, a flash of turquoise sequins, fur and swinging hair, "this is strictly between us."

"Sure thing," the girl called back. She didn't care what was going on with all these rich people; she was making a bundle.

Brad stood outside the doors under the giant awning, gasping for breath. His vision was completely gone. He couldn't drive—he didn't know if he could even make it into a taxi. His heart pounded. He had to figure out how to get out of here.

He heard the voice of one of the doormen. He could picture the man in his white pants and green, gold-braided jacket, but he couldn't see him. He could only hear him: "Anything I can help you with, Mr. Elliot?"

"No, no." Brad tried to keep the terror out of his voice. "I just stepped outside for some air."

"Some night, eh?"

"Oh, yes," Brad said, leaning against the wall and praying his vision would return. "A wonderful party."

"No, I meant the sleet."

"Sleet?" Brad repeated, and suddenly noticed the icy sound. "Ah, yes, the sleet."

"Are you sure you're all right, Mr. Elliot?"

"Yes, yes, I'm fine." He mustn't panic, he told himself.

A hand slipped under his arm, he smelled perfume and then he heard Laurie's voice, intimate in his ear. "Don't worry, Brad. I know." She raised her voice to the doorman. "I wonder if you'd be kind enough to get us a taxi?" Then she spoke quietly in Brad's ear. "Just lean on me. When I squeeze your arm, it means there's a step down. Come on. Easy does it. No one else has to know."

Brad felt relief wash over him as he allowed himself to be led away by Laurie.

Leslie was beginning to feel uncomfortable. What *was* this man Lance saying to her this time? She had already gotten rid of him twice this evening, but it seemed as if every time she turned around, there he was again, smiling easily at her and talking on and on. She wondered where Brad was. Not wanting to be rude, she kept smiling as Lance talked and laughed, but her eyes darted around the room, searching for Brad. It was strange, now that she thought about it. She hadn't seen him for quite some time.

She tried to pay attention to what Lance was saying, something about skiing in the Alps being like a Wagner aria. Good heavens, would he never stop talking long enough for her to politely excuse herself? Her eyes roved the crowd, picking out her mother and father as they talked to some people and moved on. She wondered idly where Laurie was; she hadn't seen her for some time, either.

Then the words struck her. What did she mean, she hadn't seen Laurie for some time, *either?* She hadn't seen Brad. She hadn't seen Laurie. She hadn't seen *either* of them for some time.

A low gasp escaped her lips. It had been there all along, right under her own nose. Her husband and her sister. She felt the room begin to reel.

A hand grabbed her elbow. "Mrs. Elliot?" she heard someone say. "Are you all right?" Dimly she was aware of being led away and eased down onto a nearby seat.

Brad and Laurie? It was impossible, wasn't it? Nothing was impossible, whispered a voice in her head, nothing except love. A coldness crept over her, and she felt a cold stone begin to form in her heart, felt something begin to die inside her.

Someone was patting her hand, and she heard a voice talking to her. When she blinked her eyes, she saw Lance looking at her with genuine concern in his face.

"Something wrong?" he asked anxiously.

She heard the voice come from her mouth, but it felt as if it came from someone else. Someone cold and hard. Giving him a tight little smile, she raised her eyebrows. "I told you. I drank too much champagne."

Brad picked up his suitcase and looked once more around their bedroom. His eyes filled with tears. He would never see this room again, he thought. He walked slowly down the stairs into the dining room and carefully placed the envelope on the dining room table, where he was sure Leslie would see it from the doorway.

He left all the lights burning so that Leslie wouldn't have to come home to a dark house. Oh, Leslie.

He stood in the entrance hall for one last minute, grateful that Laurie was waiting in the cab outside. Grateful that Laurie knew. Grateful to her for taking him to her apartment until he could settle his affairs in Genoa City. Grateful to her for offering to take care of Leslie, to explain everything, without mentioning his blindness.

He opened the door, turned and stared into their home once more before he stepped outside and closed the door behind him. The sound echoed in their empty home.

Leslie let herself in the front door and closed it quietly behind her, listening to the sound of her father's car driving away. She had read the note in the cloak-room, then numbly put on her coat, brushing away Lance's offer to give her a lift.

From the doorway she saw the small white envelope, stark against the highly polished dark tabletop. She was not surprised. She walked toward it, picked it up and noted that her fingers didn't shake as she opened it and took out the note.

She began to unfold the note, then stopped. Tucking it back in the envelope, she laid it carefully down on the table and left the room. She didn't bother to turn out the lights.

She walked with measured steps up the staircase, her hand barely touching the gleaming banister. Automatically she began to move toward their bedroom, but then she stopped. Her feet carried her to the guest room. She did not turn on the light. Instead, she undressed by the light that streamed in through the trees from the streetlight outside.

She dropped her clothes listlessly on a chair. When she pulled back the bedspread, she saw there were no sheets on the bed. Methodically, carefully, she walked down the hall to the linen closet and took out a set of single sheets.

As she made up the bed, her mind flashed on the bottle of pills in the medicine cabinet—the bottle that was still there from her troubled times. But her mind rejected the pills. She didn't need pills. The doctor had given her the pills because she'd been feeling too much.

That was surely not the case now, she thought, slipping into the cold narrow bed. She didn't need pills. She didn't need anything. She didn't need a nightgown. She didn't need a blanket. She didn't need food. And she didn't need sleep, she thought as she lay in bed, her eyes wide open, directed toward the ceiling but seeing nothing.

Chapter Five

Symphony of Sorrow

Laurie had never been happier. The novel she was writing seemed to spring to life on its own. She began remembering more and more details she wanted to include about Leslie's last breakdown.

Of course Laurie wouldn't publish the novel about her sister's breakdown under her own name. That would be too embarrassing for the family and for Leslie. Everyone would be mad at her if they found out. Besides, if people knew that she wrote novels based on their lives, they'd never reveal as much to her. She had changed the names, places and physical descriptions of the people. She had made the main character a dancer instead of a pianist. No one would ever guess. But she was sure this book would win her the money and the glory that was rightfully hers.

Besides feeling happy about her work, having Brad in her home had given Laurie a new lease on life. He would finally see how kind and generous she could be. He would realize that he'd chosen the wrong sister the first time around. She just had to make sure everything went according to plan. If she played her cards right, he would be hers.

THE YOUNG AND THE RESTLESS

Brad was outside learning to walk around the garden of her apartment with his eyes closed. She wanted to finish this chapter and hide it before he came back in. The way things were progressing, it wouldn't be long before she wouldn't have to hide anything. For her, there were definite advantages to loving a blind man.

It was dawn. Leslie walked barefoot into the piano room and slowly lifted the lid of the grand piano. Taking out the envelope, she sank down onto the piano bench and pulled out the note, well worn from so much rereading. She already knew it by heart, but her eyes scanned the words again.

> My dearest Leslie,
>   Although I know you won't understand, I have to leave you. I will never love another woman. I hope you will learn to love another man. If I could explain to you why I'm leaving, I wouldn't have to leave. But I can't. Perhaps I have no right to ask anything of you, but I ask only one thing—please never stop playing music. Please believe me, my darling, my love, my wife, that I am leaving out of love for you.
>   Brad

Leslie slipped the note back into its envelope, put it back under the lid of the piano and returned to the piano bench.

She began to play.

Brad was slowly adjusting to longer and longer periods of blindness. He sat now in an easy chair in Laurie's apartment, hearing sounds from outside that he'd never noticed before.

Laurie had been very good to him, very supportive and kind. When she wasn't writing, she chatted pleasantly, passing time with him as he practiced simple tasks, like climbing a flight of stairs.

But something was troubling him. "Laurie," he began, running his hand over the nubby texture of the chair's upholstery, "I think I should call Leslie. Just to see if she's all right."

He heard Laurie's voice from the opposite side of the room. "I suppose if you want to. . . ."

Eagerly he groped for the phone on the table beside him.

"Of course," Laurie went on smoothly, "hearing from you will probably make it harder on her. She's probably beginning to adjust to your not being there by now. It may stir her up if you call. But you do whatever you think is right."

His hand withdrew from the phone and settled in his lap. "You're right," he said sadly. "It's probably best if she doesn't hear from me."

He couldn't see the triumphant smile that curled the edges of Laurie's lips.

Leslie didn't hear the phone ringing at first over the loud, grand chords of her piano. But when the phone finally permeated her consciousness, her heart leaped in spite of itself. She ran to the phone and snatched it up, breathless. When she heard her father's voice, she slumped down into the chair near the telephone and listened as he told her he was calling because he hadn't seen Brad and was wondering where he was.

Leslie hadn't spoken to anyone in many days. Words seemed difficult to form. Her voice came out in measured tones. "Brad sent a telegram. His mother is ill in Chicago."

There was a momentary pause on the other end of the phone, then Stuart said he hoped everything was all right. He asked why Brad hadn't gotten in touch with him. She told him she didn't know, but that she had to practice now, and she hung up.

Stuart sat contemplatively by the phone. Then he reached for his intercom. "Gladys, be a good girl and get me Mrs. Hazel Elliot on the phone in Chicago. You'll find her number in my personal Rolodex. And when you get her on the line, hold all calls."

Brad lifted his fork to his mouth, missed by a fraction of an inch and felt the greasy smear of steak on the corner of his lip. "Damn," he muttered.

He heard Laurie's patient voice. "It's all right, Brad. It just takes practice." He heard her push away from her side of the table and smelled her perfume as she leaned close to him and began dabbing with a napkin at his mouth.

"Give me that." He tried to snatch the napkin away but couldn't quite find it.

"I'm sorry, Brad," he heard her say as she gently slipped the napkin into his hand.

"No, I'm the one who's sorry. You're being so patient with me. But it's so hard, feeling this helpless."

They continued to eat, Brad being very careful. "You know, Laurie," he began, "I've been thinking maybe it's time you talked to Leslie."

He couldn't see Laurie's one raised eyebrow. She had been waiting for this. She realized that she had to follow Brad's lead and let him dictate the timing. But finally, the moment had arrived. She kept her voice cool as she replied, "If you think so."

Brad's face took on a tender look that Laurie knew

he didn't realize was showing. Someday soon, he would look like that when he thought of her.

"Just explain to her that you've seen me, that I'm fine, and that you can't tell her what the matter is because you don't know. But please, Laurie"—he leaned forward, his face turned slightly to the left of Laurie's, pleading with the wall—"please tell her that I love her."

"Don't worry about a thing, Brad. You can leave it all in my hands."

Laurie slammed the door of her Jaguar and walked up the long winding path to Leslie's house. A light snow had fallen the night before. Other than Laurie's, there were no footsteps on the path.

As she approached the house, she heard music pouring from the room that had been added to the side of the house. She noticed something covered with snow near the front door. Drawing closer, she saw that several newspapers lay where the paper boy had tossed them, neatly enfolded in their rubber bands. A huge bouquet of large, drooping flowers, their tips snow-covered, sat by the door.

Laurie looked around to see if any neighbors were about. Quickly she knelt, took the card from the flowers out of its envelope and raised her eyebrows.

"Your music was a lovely gift. Thank you. Lance Prentiss."

Ah-ha! thought Laurie, remembering the good-looking man who had monopolized so much of Leslie's time the night of the benefit. Carefully she slid the note back in its envelope. Dear little sister must be getting a little flaky around the edges, she thought with interest. The dying flowers and piled-up newspapers in the snow were a good touch for her book, she reflected, stepping carefully over them and letting herself into the house.

"Leslie, dear," she called, pulling off her gloves and surveying the hall and living room beyond. Nothing seemed too out of place here, she noted. The music continued, a strange modern piece Laurie had never heard before.

She flung her fur on a chair and moved toward the music room, calling, "Leslie! Your sister's dropped by for a little chat." But she stopped at the entrance to the music room, stunned for one brief moment. She hadn't been prepared to see what was before her.

Leslie's hair flowed wildly around her head. She wore a slip of a nightgown in the chilly room, and her body looked painfully thin. As she slowly turned her head, having finally realized that someone was in the room, Laurie saw deep circles under her eyes.

Laurie's heart went out to her sister. Forget the book. My God, my sister is in terrible pain, she thought as she rushed toward her with outstretched arms. But Leslie pulled away from Laurie's embrace and turned back to the piano.

"Leslie," Laurie said hesitantly, "I've come to talk to you."

"Oh, really?" replied Leslie, her voice arch and cold. "What, may I ask, have you come to say?" She continued to play as she spoke. "Have you come to tell me that you've stolen my husband?"

Laurie gasped, truly frightened now. Had Leslie's madness made her clairvoyant? How could she possibly know that Brad was with her?

"What's the matter, lovely little conniving sister of mine?" Leslie's voice was chilling. "Don't know what to say? Cat got your tongue? Can't talk your way out of this one?" The strange, dissonant chords continued to flow from the piano.

"Leslie," Laurie said, "you don't know what you're saying. You're not yourself."

"I am more myself than I have ever been," Leslie said haughtily, her normally cultured tone now imperious. "Why don't you just run along now, you petty little thief. You've gotten what you always wanted. Take him. You can have him. He'll never love you the way he loves me." Leslie's hand darted out, flicked a page of music and returned to the keyboard. "There will come a day when he wants to come crawling back to me. But the door will be shut. So enjoy him now, while you can. He won't be interested in the likes of you for long."

Laurie felt impotent anger well up within her, and her breath came out in short gasps as she realized that Leslie had bested her once again. But then, just as suddenly, her eyes narrowed to slits at a second realization: her sister had saved her the trouble of lying. She had come prepared to tell Leslie that Brad no longer loved her. But now she could go back to Brad and say that Leslie didn't want him back. None of it would be lies. Brad would know that she was telling the truth. Because it would *be* true, it would ring true in her voice. She could even say that there had been flowers from Lance. She could say that Leslie had been playing the piano, rehearsing as usual. And Brad would fall gratefully into her waiting arms.

"Thank you, Leslie," she said, her composure regained. "You've made this conversation so much easier."

For a moment Leslie stopped playing and looked at her sister. Laurie couldn't meet Leslie's direct, piercing gaze. Then Leslie snorted and turned back to the piano. "You mean thank you for saving you from becoming a liar as well as a cheat." She began to play again, furiously.

Laurie quickly left the house. Her sister's perceptions were uncanny—she wanted to be far away, fast.

Leslie listened for the click of the door. She braced herself, biting her lip. She mustn't show anything, she told herself. For all she knew, Laurie could even be spying on her, peeking in the window. No, she couldn't show anything, to anyone, ever. She couldn't show that her heart was breaking—breaking, cracking, crumbling.

Let them think she was crazy. Maybe she was. Let them all think anything they wanted, as long as they didn't know and couldn't see the pain, the hurt, the terrible misery.

She couldn't go on without Brad. But she had to. She would continue to play and allow a callus to form around her heart. She would never again let anyone close to her, never again allow anyone into her life. She would play music.

And she would never love again.

Chapter Six

Too Late

While Laurie was at Leslie's, Brad began to think. He thought of Snapper telling him he was making a mistake. Of Barbara saying lies and love didn't mix. He heard Leslie's voice, pleading with him, saying she could bear anything, that they could face anything together, that all he had to do was trust her enough to tell her the truth.

His mind went back to the conversation they'd had in the living room. But now that he thought about it, hadn't it been an idle conversation? The kind of thing said in the heat of romance? Leslie was right: she'd said love was more than romance, and that if he truly loved her, he'd tell her.

My Lord, he thought, he'd been a fool. How could he have even imagined that she wouldn't be there for him? They could face this together. They had come through her breakdown together. She was much stronger now. They could come through this, too. Together.

He would be firm, that was all. He would simply insist that she continue with her career. It was only foolish pride keeping him from her, not wanting to be helpless or a burden to her. But he was already becoming competent at moving around. Now that the blindness was almost complete, it wasn't even that frightening anymore. It was the unknown that had been so terrifying.

For the first time in months, he smiled—*really* smiled—easing the lines of care etched into his brow. What relief he felt. He'd go to Leslie on bended knee and beg her forgiveness. If she would take him back, somewhat damaged and a bit awkward, he thought wryly, he wanted to come home. Home to Leslie, to his love.

He sat on Laurie's couch, his newly trained ears straining for the familiar sound of her car. He couldn't wait until she got back so he could get in the car and go home.

The delivery boy whistled as he hopped out of the front seat, went around the back of the van and slid the big bouquet toward him carefully. Mrs. Elliot was one of the most famous people in Genoa City. Straightening his black tie and pulling his short tan uniform jacket down smartly, he hoisted the flowers and strode up the path.

As he neared the house, he saw the flowers he'd left two days ago, still sitting by the door. Maybe somebody was sick, he thought. Maybe that was why these flowers were arriving. He looked around him, confused. Should he deliver them or take them back to the shop? He shrugged. It wasn't any of his business. He was a delivery boy. If somebody yelled, "Deliver!" he hollered, "Where to?"

As he stooped to put the flowers down, he heard music coming from the side of the house. Pretty weird, he thought, straightening. Some modern stuff. Well, at least he could say he'd heard the famous Mrs. Brooks-Elliot playing in person, he thought importantly as he whistled his way back down the path.

It was four A.M. Leslie pulled another maroon leather-covered box off the shelf in the den. Each box had her initials, a city and a date inscribed in gold lettering. She wouldn't allow herself to think about the evening Brad had come bursting through the front door carrying a packing case, saying that he'd had a wonderful thing made especially for her so that she could keep mementos of every concert she played.

She didn't have time to think about Brad now. She had to remember which city it had been. All those hotels and dressing rooms looked exactly alike. This had been the one where she'd slept alone. Which was it? Remember, Leslie, she told herself. She tried to picture the room. What had been out the window? Mountains! That was it, it had been Denver.

She reached up for the Denver box, pulled it down and began rummaging through the pile of telegrams. There it was. Hurriedly she put everything away except for the one telegram, which she took downstairs and placed carefully on top of the piano. There. Done. Now they'd all think she'd snapped. And if they thought that, maybe they'd tiptoe around the whole issue of Brad, not wanting to upset her. That way, she could hide everything she felt.

As she left the room, she automatically turned out the light. But then she stopped, thought and turned it back on. Might as well leave all the lights on: that would help convince people.

As she crawled back into the narrow single bed in the guestroom, where there was no one to see her and no one to convince that she wasn't feeling right, she felt the tears begin. Immediately she got out of bed and went down the stairs to her music room. Play, she told herself, play music. Only in the mighty chords and delicate arpeggios of her music did she feel safe enough to let her feelings show.

Stuart brought his Mercedes to a quick halt in front of Leslie's house. Something was wrong. He didn't know what, but he knew something was wrong.

His eyes narrowed, and he pulled his sunglasses off to get a good look at the front of her house. What the devil was going on around here? he thought, running toward the house, stepping over the newspapers, brushing past the flowers and rushing in the door.

"Leslie?" he called out, heading for the music room. Her piano playing spilled out of the room, a haunting, eerie piece he'd never heard her play before.

He didn't pause for a moment when he reached the door and saw her small frame, her wild hair lit by the sun that filtered in through the windows. In three strides he was across the room and had her in his arms, rocking her, crooning, "Leslie, my darling daughter." She felt small to him, like the child she'd once been, and as he hugged her frail body, he felt a giant protectiveness rise up within him for this lovely, delicate daughter of his.

She pulled away. If her eyes hadn't been so haggard and rimmed by deep circles—but somehow blazingly beautiful—her voice would never have given her away as she said coolly, "Hello, Father." She turned from him and said evenly, "I'm practicing." She began playing again.

Stuart stood, wondering how to proceed. He knew

from the last time that he had to go very cautiously. But damn it all, this was his daughter. He'd take the bull by the horns and let the cards fall where they may.

"Leslie, you don't seem very well."

"I'm fine, Father," she said, not looking at him.

He sat down on the piano bench next to her. "New piece you're playing?" he asked.

"Yes, it's Shostakovich. I've always found him a bit discordant, but he suits my mood quite well at the moment."

Stuart listened in silence for a few moments. Finally, he said quietly, "I haven't heard from or seen Brad in a while."

"He's in Chicago. He sent a telegram. His mother's ill," Leslie said, enunciating the words carefully.

"Yes, you mentioned that on the phone." Stuart hesitated but finally continued, feeling that truth was the most important thing right now. "I called his mother. She said he wasn't there." He held his breath, waiting to see how Leslie would respond.

She acted as if she hadn't heard him, merely nodded her head toward the telegram lying on top of the piano. "There's the telegram, Father. You can see for yourself."

Stuart rose and picked up the telegram. As he read, he didn't see Leslie glance at him surreptitiously. When his eyes happened to fall on the date, he uttered an exclamation of surprise. "But Leslie!" he burst out. "This is several months old!"

"Oh, is it? I wouldn't really know."

"Leslie, can you stop playing for a minute and talk to me?" he asked, putting his arm around her shoulder.

She stopped and sat stiffly, staring straight ahead.

"Leslie, daughter of mine," Stuart said, drawing her close to him on the piano bench. "Don't you think you'd like to tell your dad what's going on?"

She leaned against him. His body felt big and strong. She could smell his after-shave lotion, and memories of childhood washed over her. She wanted to bury her head in his shoulder, wanted to call out, "Daddy, Daddy, I can't go on. Why wasn't I good enough? Why doesn't he love me? What did I do to turn him away from me?" But as she felt herself softening, she felt tears begin. And she knew that if she began to cry, she would never stop.

Stuart felt the moment pass, felt her stiffen again, felt he had failed her.

"There's nothing going on," she said.

Stuart heard her words with a heavy heart. But if he couldn't reach her emotionally at the moment, he was still her father. At least he could provide for her until he could think of what else to do. As her hands began to reach for the piano keys again, he reached out and stopped her.

"Leslie, have you been eating?" he asked.

"I really wouldn't know, Father."

"Have you been sleeping?"

"I suppose so. People do sleep."

Stuart reached a quick decision. "Listen, dear, can you hear me?"

"Of course I can," she snapped. "I haven't gone deaf. I've just gone mad."

Stuart drew back. Leslie had never snapped at him in her whole life. He needed help. He needed the best doctors money could buy, he needed someone trained to deal with this kind of thing. But in the meantime, he would attend to his daughter the best way he knew how.

"Leslie, I'm going to hire someone to come and

stay with you. To prepare meals for you, and make sure your laundry gets done, and just . . . well . . . come and keep you company."

"That's a very good idea, Father."

"It is?" He'd expected her to balk.

"Yes. It's so much more reasonable to *pay* someone to care for you. It's more honest that way, don't you think?"

Stuart was frightened by the hard edge in her voice.

Brad's sensitive ears caught the sound of Laurie's Jaguar as it purred up to the curb. He listened with delight as he heard the car door close and waited for the sound of her key in the front door lock. He smiled a broad, happy smile as he heard her let herself into the apartment, throw her keys down, take off her coat and stop for a moment in front of what he guessed must be the hall mirror. Funny, he mused, how people primp. He wouldn't know if she had a colander on her head. Oh, how wonderful he felt. He could even find humor in the world again.

"How'd it go?" he called out happily.

He heard Laurie take a deep breath and wondered what she was bracing herself for. He heard the soft sound of her boots coming across the carpet and felt the weight as she sat down next to him on the couch and took his hand.

"What is it?" he asked, confusion and worry welling up inside him. "Is she all right? Oh, no! She's not. Of course she's not. She's broken down again, hasn't she?" The questions tumbled from his mouth. It hit him how horribly selfish he'd been, thinking he was protecting her when in fact he'd harmed her— perhaps irreparably.

Laurie said quietly, "She's rehearsing. She said she's never felt more like herself."

There was a stunned silence in the room. Brad's mind reeled.

Laurie congratulated herself on not having said that Leslie was fine. That was a lie. If she could just stick to the literal truth, and leave out all the shading, this would go fine.

"I see. . . ." Brad's voice was tight. "What else did she say?"

Laurie paused. This part was difficult. "Brad, maybe it would be better if you didn't know exactly what she said."

"What did she say, Laurie?" Brad demanded.

"I'd prefer to not say. I'd prefer to just leave it that . . . that . . ."

"That what?" Brad shouted.

He felt Laurie move nearer to him, felt her press herself up against his arm, smelled her perfume and felt her lips almost brushing his ear as she murmured, "Don't think about it anymore, Brad. It's all right. We have each other now. Just allow these feelings that have been growing between us to develop. I didn't want to do anything before, but now . . ."

Brad flung Laurie away from him and leaped up from the couch, knocking into a magazine basket nearby. He kicked out at it but missed. "I have no idea what *you* think has been 'developing' between us, Laurie," he said with tight-lipped fury. "Now tell me what my wife said."

The word "wife" hurt Laurie harder than his rough hands as he'd pushed her away. They would never see that she was somebody, she thought bitterly. The two of them so high and mighty. They were more together even when they were apart than she'd ever been with anyone. She didn't care about either of them. She wanted them out of her life.

"I was going to soften the words for you, you ingrate," she spat out, "but now I think I'll just tell you exactly what your precious *wife* said. *And I quote.* She said, 'When he comes crawling back, the door will be shut.'"

Laurie watched as Brad staggered and reached out for something to grab on to. She'd be damned if she'd help him. She'd helped enough, and where had it gotten her? He'd pushed her roughly in her own home. Let him stumble and grope his way right out of here.

"You're lying," he said between clenched teeth.

"The hell I am," she said self-righteouslessly.

And Brad could hear the terrible ring of truth in her hateful words.

Stuart's secretary said that Brad Elliot was on the phone. Stuart said, "Hold all calls," and snatched up the phone.

"Stuart?" Brad said tentatively, but Stuart cut him off.

"I don't give a damn what's going on with you," he said levelly into the phone. "If you so much as step foot in this office or go near my daughter, I swear by all I hold dear, I'll murder you with my bare hands. And that goes for Genoa City, too. Clear out, Elliot, you miserable hypocrite with all your fancy talk about honor." He slammed down the phone and felt the blood raging through his temples.

Brad had somehow gotten himself into a taxi and into the Genoa City Hotel. His hands shook as he reached for the phone. Carefully he felt for each number that he used to dial without even thinking.

The phone rang and rang. Finally, he heard Leslie's voice, although it sounded strange. He couldn't say anything for a moment. When he heard her begin to hang up, he cried, "Wait, Leslie, don't hang up!"

She didn't say anything, but he could hear her breath over the phone. He held the phone close to his face, embracing it. Oh, how he yearned to reach out and touch her face, her hair! But she didn't want him. He could beg. But no, she didn't want him. An ugly scene was the last thing he wanted. Besides, he couldn't bear to have the last words she ever said to him be words of rejection. He had to make this simple and direct.

"Leslie, I've called to ask you for a divorce."

There was a silence on the other end of the phone.

Leslie held the phone close to her face, caressing it, wishing she could say, "Come home, Brad. I need you and love you. I can forgive anything, if you'll just come home." But no, she'd never let her feelings show to anyone again. Instead, she let her words come out in even, measured tones.

"All right, Brad."

There was another silence. Each of them wanted to cry. Each of them wanted to say, "Take me back." Each of them wanted the other more than anything in the world.

The silence dragged on.

"I don't think we have anything else to say to one another, Brad."

"No, I suppose we don't."

"You can communicate with me through lawyers from now on," Leslie said.

"All right," Brad answered.

"Good-bye, Brad," Leslie said, biting her lip, not wanting him to hear the catch in her voice.

"Leslie! This is wrong!" Brad called out, but she had already hung up.

He checked his breast pocket for the airline ticket resting there, then called the desk for a cab, picked up his suitcase and made his way to the door with the cane he had begun using a few days before. He tapped his way along the hall until he heard the metal clang of the elevator doors. When he found the elevator button, he pushed it and waited for the sound of the opening doors. He got in, found the bottom button and felt the elevator carry him to the lobby. Then he tapped his way across the lobby, accepting the bellboy's help, and allowed the doorman to help him into a cab.

He asked the driver to take him to the airport. As they pulled away from the curb, Brad said, "I wonder if you'd mind stopping at one address for a moment?"

The cab smoothly took the familiar curves of the street where he'd lived and soon pulled up in front of his house. "I won't be long," Brad said. Opening the door himself, he took a few steps along the path, with the aid of his cane . . . then stopped.

Snow had begun to fall; it felt cool on his raised face. He stood there and tried to remember all the smells, all the sights he'd known so well. He tried to set indelibly in his mind the winding path, the big maple tree, the manicured lawn, the shutters, the brass doorknob, the big bay windows of the living room and the glass enclosed den that he had designed and had built for Leslie.

He heard the music. Heard Leslie's lovely music pouring out into the snow and the night from the room he'd built for her. He recognized the piece; he must've heard her play it a million times. It was a heart-breaking strain from Tchaikovsky's *Romeo and Juliet*.

He allowed the music to wash over him. He told himself that she wasn't playing it for any special reason—it was just one of the pieces in her repertoire. Laurie had said that Leslie was rehearsing.

He listened to Leslie's beautiful music for another moment, then turned, tapped his way back into the taxi and sat stonily in the backseat as it rushed him off to the airport and away from Genoa City forever.

Chapter Seven

Wounds Heal Slowly

Miss Wakefield sat in Leslie's kitchen knitting contentedly as the lovely piano music filled the entire house. A small smile graced her homely face, and she nodded her graying head to the music. Her stubby fingers flew as yet another thick, dark sweater for her nephew in England slowly inched its way to life. One sturdy shoe tapped time to the music on the kitchen floor, which shone to her satisfaction. The young girl she'd hired to do the heavy cleaning was shaping up nicely under her watchful eye.

At first she had been reluctant to accept the job. Mental disturbances were not her specialty, she had informed Mr. Brooks politely, and she couldn't imagine why the agency had even troubled to give him her number. But he'd mentioned how very happy and grateful her last employer's family had been with her. May she rest in peace, poor old soul, thought Miss Wakefield, tears forming as they did every time she thought of the old lady she'd worked for for eight years. Mr. Brooks had said that frankly he was desperate, and he didn't want a nurse. He wanted someone to care for his daughter.

The feeling in his voice when he'd said the word "care" had touched Miss Wakefield. And although she had been looking forward to returning to England, her home, she'd finally accepted the job. After all, she'd had nothing else lined up. And besides, these Americans certainly did pay handsomely.

Now, as she sat knitting, she felt that she'd been right to accept. Over the last months, she'd fattened Leslie up a bit, although she was still a thin little wisp of a thing. She'd seen to it that those dreadful circles had disappeared from under Leslie's eyes. She'd made sure that the poor child was in bed every night by eleven, although the first month or so had been a bit of a battle, with Leslie haunting the house at all hours of the night and day like a little ghost. But eventually, Miss Wakefield thought with pride, her nightly glasses of hot milk laced with brandy had worked. Now, Leslie was back on a normal schedule.

The maestro had helped, too, of course. Miss Wakefield would never dream of not giving credit where credit was due. He arrived punctually every morning at nine and disappeared with Leslie into the music room, from where Miss Wakefield could hear his passionate tenor voice crooning, "Slower, more delicately," or booming, "Brava! *Magnifique!*" Miss Wakefield prepared their meals, made sure the house was as neat as a pin and did her best to see that Leslie wasn't lonely.

No one had explained to her exactly what the trouble was, but she'd guessed from the first that there must be a man problem. The house definitely looked as if there'd been a man in it quite recently. In the first week, during one of Leslie's predawn haunts to the piano room, Miss Wakefield had come tiptoeing down the steps, not wanting to frighten the child but trying to figure out how to get her back in bed. She'd seen Leslie take something out of the piano. After she'd gotten her back in bed, she'd slipped back down the stairs and, feeling that snooping was in this case justified, had read the note.

Miss Wakefield's heart had gone out to Leslie. Poor little thing, he'd left her; think of it! For the life of her, she couldn't imagine why. It seemed so obvious from his letter that he loved her. Well, the workings of the human heart were strange, Miss Wakefield thought, shrugging. She, of course, had never married after poor Rupert . . . But she mustn't think about that. Wars were terrible things. She'd made out all right, though, hadn't she? She was lucky to have loved once, and she decided that she'd never love anyone but him. Not to mention that after the war there were so many more women than eligible men. She'd settled very nicely into her work, thank you very much, and now she allowed herself to enjoy the doings of younger folks.

The doorbell rang, and she glanced at her watch. Right on time, she thought, a little smile curling her lips. Whoever this Mr. Lance Prentiss was, he was certainly much more than a music fan of Leslie's. Every single day for months, at precisely eleven A.M., a huge bouquet of flowers arrived from him. If Miss Wakefield had her way, she'd see this Mr. Prentiss before too long. He must be quite well off, considering how much he'd spent on flowers alone in the last few months.

She put down her knitting and went to the door.

Rio de Janeiro. São Paulo. Caracas. Bogotá. The very names of the cities dazzled Miss Wakefield. To think that she should ever be in cities as exotic as these!

She fluttered and flapped through city after city, making sure Leslie's things were packed properly, making sure the hotels were expecting them and making sure a nice glass of warm milk was placed beside Leslie's bed every evening.

The maestro snapped his fingers at porters and smartly supervised the lighting of each great hall. He personally tuned every piano.

And through every city they moved during the South American tour, Leslie played magnificently. She read the reviews listlessly, picked at her food, and graciously accepted Miss Wakefield's ministrations. But late at night, after Miss Wakefield had finally bustled out of her room, calling, "Make sure you drink your milk, dear," Leslie lay in bed, wide-eyed, staring at the ceiling and wishing Brad were by her side.

On street corner after street corner, in nameless city after city throughout America, young women stopped and nudged one another as the tall, erect man tapped his way past them, his handsome face clearly bearing a grief greater than blindness.

Leslie stared out from the terrace doors of her suite in the lavish Mexico City Hilton. Below her the city teemed with life. Buses, taxis and cars zigzagged through the wide boulevard. Crowds pushed along the sidewalks. The gay sound of the mariachi band in the plaza rose above the honking horns and filtered its way into the hotel suite.

Miss Wakefield's knitting needles clacked away, and occasionally she let out little clucks and murmurs of approval, as the maestro read from the *Mexico City Tribune* in his magnificent voice:

As all of Mrs. Elliot's fans know, her playing has always shown great skill. But in her recent season, it has taken on a new maturity. There is an exquisite, haunting quality to the music that is rare to find in any pianist, not to mention such a young performer, and a woman at that. Her repertoire has expanded greatly, including new, daring pieces by modern composers. Mrs. Elliot manages to lend grace and melody to music that often seems incomprehensible.

We of Mexico City are proud that she has come here to grace our city, and we look forward to hearing every concert of her two-week stay.

We accept with great regret that Mrs. Elliot has declined to meet with any of us, since we would like to open the gates of our city wide to her. But we respect her wishes and feel grateful that she will share, if not her lovely presence socially, at least her lovely music in this guest appearance that shows every sign of being the finest our fair city has ever known.

The maestro finished reading with a grand flourish and adjusted his ascot. At last he had found a pianist worthy of his great talent as a coach. But he didn't want to appear immodest.

"Of course, Leslie, you have great talent," he said, swelling his chest, "but I think we must thank the one who deserves the real credit for this spectacular series."

Leslie continued staring out the window. She was used to the maestro's pomposity, and, in fact, it mildly amused her. She could put up with certain flaws in his character because he was very helpful to her.

The maestro paused for effect. "I think we have to thank Miss Wakefield for all her help."

Miss Wakefield's eyebrows shot up, and she began

to sputter. Then she saw that the maestro was joking. "Oh, go on," she said, waving her hand and blushing in spite of herself.

Just then there was a knock at the door, and Miss Wakefield rose to answer it. A bellhop handed her a letter on a tray. She tipped him and glanced at the letter with curiosity. "It's for you, Leslie. It's marked 'personal.'"

Leslie's heart leaped. Brad, oh, finally! she thought, rushing from the window. She took the letter, glanced at the handwriting and frowned. It wasn't Brad's. She handed it back to Miss Wakefield and slowly returned to the window.

The maestro and Miss Wakefield exchanged glances. Through unspoken consent, neither had ever mentioned the missing husband. Miss Wakefield didn't want to pry, but she felt it important that Leslie reenter life. She looked at the maestro questioningly, and he nodded.

She cleared her throat a few times and nervously straightened the bow on her collar. The maestro waved her on. Finally she said, "Dear, don't you even want to read this?"

"No," Leslie replied quietly.

"But dear—"

"It's probably from a fan. You know I never read their letters before a performance."

"Yes, but dear, none of the fans ever mark their letters 'personal.'"

Leslie didn't answer her.

"It's very good quality paper," Miss Wakefield said, hefting the letter. "It's really rather intriguing, don't you think? Like a little mystery."

Leslie was becoming exasperated. "If you're so interested in it, open it yourself."

"Oh, my dear, I couldn't do that."

"Yes, you could."

"Oh, no, I couldn't."

"Please, Miss Wakefield!" Leslie was ready to do anything to stop this interminable talking. "Please, open the letter!"

"Well, if you insist," she said, curiosity overtaking her. Carefully she opened the letter and read it to herself. How very interesting, she thought, smiling. Now, if there were just some way she could rouse Leslie's interest.

"Oh, well, I'm sure you wouldn't be interested in this," she said, winking at the maestro. "You haven't seemed the least interested in this person in all these months."

From the window, Leslie asked, "What person?"

"The gentleman who sent you flowers every day when we were in Genoa City."

Leslie thought of Lance. For the first few weeks, in her terrible state, she had ignored the flowers. But slowly, she'd begun to feel pleased every morning when the doorbell rang. She'd told herself that it was nothing more than giving in to flattery. But the truth was that she was lonely, feeling like a prisoner in the very world she had created. Miss Wakefield was very good to her, and the maestro was an excellent coach, filling her need to engross herself in music. But in her heart, there was a loneliness for her own kind.

"What does he say?" she asked, trying to feign indifference.

Miss Wakefield felt ecstatic, but she didn't allow it to show in her voice. "It's a very polite letter. He says he happens to be in Mexico City on business and read that you were playing here. Then, by chance, he learned that you were staying in the same hotel. He says that he doesn't know anyone here, and wondered if you'd think it rude if he presumed on your having met only once to invite you to dinner. It's a very polite letter, really. Most proper."

Leslie thought of the dinners she spent with Miss Wakefield and the maestro. Miss Wakefield chattered away, the maestro added stentorian comments from time to time and Leslie ate her meal silently before returning alone to her room.

"Shall I write a little note saying you're not quite up to it, dear?" Miss Wakefield held her breath, hoping she hadn't gone too far.

"No. See if he's free tomorrow night after my concert."

The maestro beamed, but Miss Wakefield tried to keep her voice expressionless as she picked up the phone.

Lance threw a white dinner jacket down and pulled a loose-knit sweater over his head. He looked in the mirror, shook his head, ripped the sweater off, threw it across the room and stood staring in the hotel closet.

This was absurd, he thought. He was like a schoolboy on his first date. What was happening to him? He'd never in his life thought about what to wear, instead always reaching for whatever felt comfortable. And whatever felt comfortable turned out to be appropriate, always. Until tonight.

He hoped she wouldn't ask him too many questions about his business in Mexico City. His company had a branch here that ran perfectly without him— probably better, in fact, than when he was here, he thought ruefully. The only reason he'd traveled all this distance was to see Leslie.

He'd gone through hell and high water to get her itinerary. Then he'd paid a small fortune buying off hotel clerks until he'd finally found the hotel where she was staying. It had cost him double to get a room here thanks to the clerk, who obviously had a nose for who would pay what to do what.

Ah, well, he thought, it was a small price to pay for the chance to see her again.

He was frankly surprised at himself about this whole infatuation. Over the past few months, he'd found that he couldn't get Leslie out of his mind. He dated his usual round of leggy showgirls and passionate intellectuals, cool society beauties and willing waitresses. Before this, the variety had been the spice, the hunt always more interesting than the catch. But lately he'd become more and more dissatisfied. He'd found one date was plenty, where previously only a month of wining and dining had sufficed. And he'd felt compelled to place a monthly order with the Genoa City florist.

He had even gone so far as to send one of the bright young men employed by his company to snoop around Genoa City. Lance had noted that his heart had begun to pound when the underling had reported that from all he could gather, Leslie's husband was gone, and Leslie had become a recluse. Town gossip ranged wildly from another woman—even possibly Leslie's sister—to some secret disease. But all Lance was really interested in at present was that her husband was not around.

He was sure that this dinner date could be nothing but profoundly disappointing. She couldn't possibly live up to all his expectations and fantasies. But, he shrugged, he'd certainly wasted more time and money on lots of other women. At least this one could play the piano. Finally he settled on a raw silk sport coat and navy slacks.

Leslie felt strangely unsettled. She wasn't sure exactly why she had accepted the dinner date, other than a normal yen for company. But why was she having so much trouble deciding just what to wear? Finally, trying not to let anything show in her voice, she asked Miss Wakefield to be kind enough to lay out something for dinner. She was so preoccupied about her concert, she said offhandedly, that she couldn't take the time to decide about anything as petty as what to wear to a dinner that she didn't want to go to in the first place.

After the concert, the ovations and the encore, Leslie went back to her suite to change. She was in the bedroom slipping into the pale blue sheath that Miss Wakefield had chosen when the doorbell rang.

Miss Wakefield felt butterflies in her stomach. When she opened the door, she had to keep from gasping in involuntary admiration. Heavens, this Mr. Prentiss was a handsome one, she thought. He was also a real gentleman, someone who knew how to talk to her without being too familiar or too cold, she noted as they chatted until Leslie was ready. Miss Wakefield noticed that Lance was nervous, although he hid it well. She also noticed that when Leslie entered the room, she carried herself a little straighter than usual and seemed incredibly cool—except that her cheeks were flushed.

As Miss Wakefield waved them down the hall, she thought what a handsome couple they made, he so broad, blond and handsome, she so slender, dark and beautiful.

Lance took Leslie's elbow and said that he hoped she didn't mind, but he'd made reservations in the hotel restaurant; that way, they wouldn't be out too late. Coolly she told him that it was fine. They rode the elevator in silence to the top floor, and the doors opened onto a lovely, large, crowded room that looked down on Mexico City.

The restaurant was lit with candles that glowed from small red glass containers set on tables of dark carved wood. The table linens were red, the floor was tiled with terra-cotta, and there was a huge brick hearth. All in all, the place had a very cozy, peasant-like look, even though the elegant service included several waiters for each table.

They followed the maître d' to a table near the windows and sat facing one another, neither knowing what to say. Lance felt at a complete loss. Not since he'd been fourteen years old had he not known what to say to a woman—any woman, no matter what her age or social class. He felt desperate.

"Lovely view," he finally managed, and could've kicked himself for saying such an uninspired thing.

"Yes," Leslie agreed, looking out at the twinkling lights of Mexico City. She had never liked dates, even when she was a young girl. Only with Brad had she felt comfortable from the first. But she musn't think about Brad.

Both were relieved when a waiter appeared asking them what they would like to drink. Lance felt he could use a double shot of tequila to loosen things up. He raised his eyebrows questioningly to Leslie.

"I'd like some mineral water, please," she said.

Drat, thought Lance. A dilemma. Should he order a drink anyway? No, that would be rude. He'd have to face this stone cold sober. "Make that two, waiter."

THE YOUNG AND THE RESTLESS

The waiter placed large red leather menus with gold tassels before them and left the table, shaking his head. He would never understand Americans.

Leslie and Lance busied themselves studying the menu as the waiter brought a carafe of water with lemon slices. Lance was surprised to note that the idea of food seemed unappetizing. What was going on with him?

When another waiter came to take their order, Leslie murmured that the hour was late and she'd just like some broiled chicken and a salad. Lance ordered the same for himself, and again they sat, neither knowing what to say. Finally Lance blurted out, "I don't know why, but I really can't think of a thing to say."

Leslie looked at him with such a grateful expression that he was encouraged. "I can't, either," she admitted, and the tension between them seemed to ease a bit.

"It was very nice of you to join me this evening," Lance said. "Sometimes these business trips get a bit lonely." Why had he said that? he wondered. Why wasn't he making easy, light, witty conversation with this woman? What power did she have to make his usually silver tongue turn to lead?

Leslie found herself wanting to pour her heart out to this man, stranger that he was, to say that, yes, she felt a terrible loneliness lately. But the words wouldn't come, as if she had an internal mechanism forcing her mouth shut, warning her never let anyone know what she was really feeling. So, to get off the topic, she asked about his business.

When most women inquired into his professional life, Lance generally lied and told them he ran guns or smuggled drugs. They would laugh, and the conversation would go on to other subjects. But this time, with Leslie, he found himself talking about his role as an industrialist, even going to far as to explain that his factories primarily manufactured ball bearings, metal closures, and industrial tools for tool and die works. She asked him questions, and he noticed that they were serious, thoughtful inquiries about how this machine worked or why that metal functioned better than another.

Their food came, and they continued to talk. He asked about her concerts, about how she chose which pieces to play, and they talked at length about classical music, with which Lance showed an amazing familiarity. Both were surprised at how fast the meal seemed to go, how quickly the waiter brought fruit. Then they refused coffee, and the check arrived.

Although they kept the conversation on neutral territory, Lance had to restrain himself from asking where her husband was. As the waiter came and collected the check, Lance was floored by the fact that his brain would not give him one clever way to say he'd like to see her again. She seemed to him like a butterfly or a beam of light, something that would disappear if he trod too hard. He felt foolish and tongue-tied, and all the usual smooth ways of suggesting a second date sounded cheap to his mind.

He was still desperately seeking a way to say he'd like to see her again as he escorted her out of the restaurant, into the elevator and down the hall to her room. And he still didn't know what to say as she held out her hand, thanked him for a pleasant dinner and slipped into her room.

As her door quietly clicked shut, Lance stood in the hall open-mouthed. There was only one explanation, he thought, his hand tingling from the contact with hers. He'd fallen in love.

Leslie leaned against the closed door, trying to still her pounding heart. She'd found it so easy to talk to him that it disturbed her. She didn't want anyone in her life; her music was enough. Still, it had been so pleasant to have dinner with someone who didn't seem to want anything from her except her company.

Miss Wakefield was always watching her out of the corner of her eye, making sure she was all right. The maestro always paid such close attention to her every mood, constantly worried about how it might affect her playing. But finally, tonight, she'd had a simple, normal dinner, with no emotional attachments.

Yes, but if there were no emotional attachments, asked a voice inside her head, why are you feeling so flustered? She didn't like this feeling. She didn't want any emotional hubbub, didn't want any feelings at all. If he called again, she would have Miss Wakefield tell him politely that her concerts were too draining to allow for another dinner.

At a second-rate hotel in a rundown section of Pittsburgh, the ladies of the night, the gambling men and the traveling salesmen all wondered what was up with the handsome blind man who sat in his room day after day listening over and over to the record of some fancy-dance classical piano music.

The day after their date, Lance wanted to call and ask Leslie for dinner. But something stopped him. Instead, he went to her concert.

Her music was exquisite, there was no question of that. But as Lance watched her slender body move gracefully with the music, what he noticed most was

Soaps & Serials™ Fans!

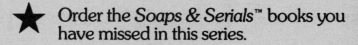

★ Order the *Soaps & Serials*™ books you have missed in this series.

★ Collect other *Soaps & Serials*™ series from their very beginnings.

★ Give *Soaps & Serials*™ series as gifts to other fans.

...see other side for ordering information

You can now order previous titles of *Soaps & Serials*™ Books by mail!

Just complete the order form, detach, and send together with your check or money order payable to:

Soaps & Serials™
120 Brighton Road, Box 5201
Clifton, NJ 07015-5201

--- --- --- --- --- --- --- --- --- ---

Please <u>circle</u> the book #'s you wish to order:

The Young and The Restless	1	2	3	4	5	6	7
Days of Our Lives	1	2	3	4	5	6	7
Guiding Light	1	2	3	4	5	6	7
Another World	1	2	3	4	5	6	7
As The World Turns	1	2	3	4	5	6	7
Dallas™	1	2	3	4	5	6	7
Knots Landing™	1	2	3	4	5	6	7
Capitol™	1	2	3	4	NOT AVAILABLE		

Each book is $2.50 ($3.50 in Canada).

Total number of books
circled _____ × price above = $ _____ .

Sales tax (CT and NY residents only) $ _____ .

Shipping and Handling $ _____ .95

Total payment enclosed $ _____ .
(check or money orders only)

Name _____

Address _____ Apt# _____

City _____

State _____ Zip _____

Telephone (_____) _____
Area code   YR 7

the passion that emanated from her—the deep, deep passion, hidden when she spoke. When they had sat opposite one another in the restaurant, she had allowed no emotion to show, only good breeding and polite manners. But as he watched her play, her chestnut hair gleaming under the lights and her frail body swaying to the music, he began to feel a lust overtake him, a lust in response to the great passion he saw within her. Where he had felt strangely attracted to her sensitivity before, he now felt a carnal desire that was stronger than anything he'd ever experienced. He wanted to touch her, to slip that elegant black dress off her creamy white shoulders and have it drop to the floor. He wanted to take the pins from her hair, one by one, and run his hands through those long, luxuriant curls. He wanted to smell her breath and feel her breasts press against him. He wanted to touch her in whatever way it took to make her body thrill to him the way it was now, on stage, under the lights, swaying to the lovely music and inflaming him.

Easy boy, he told himself. Easy now, or you'll fall in love for real.

When Lance didn't call the next day, Leslie felt despondent. You see, she told herself, that's what happens. The moment you let anyone in, you get hurt. So she closed her heart, absolutely determined to refuse his invitation. If it came.

The following day, a woman with a thick Mexican accent called Leslie's room, saying she was Mr. Prentiss's secretary. She said he had called from Guadalajara, where his business had taken him, and that he would be back in Mexico City tomorrow evening. If Mrs. Elliot was free, he'd like to have dinner with her.

Leslie shook her head and told Miss Wakefield to say no. Miss Wakefield covered the phone with her hand and whispered, "Now you can't tell me, dear, that you'd honestly prefer my boring company and the maestro's to such a handsome young man, who's as much a stranger in this city as you are."

Leslie studied Miss Wakefield. So, she thought, the woman wasn't quite as scatterbrained and foolish as she let on. Leslie gave a little half smile, a shrug and nodded her head in assent.

Miss Wakefield's voice was calmer than she felt when she replied that Mrs. Elliot would be available.

So the hot days and cool nights passed in Mexico City. Leslie played every night. Lance made his secretary lie every other day, saying that he was here or there, when in fact he was holed up in his hotel room, ordering room service meals and stiffer orders from the hotel bar, feeling his passion for Leslie grow even though he carefully refrained from touching any more of her than her elbow as he escorted her in and out of the hotel restaurant.

But he didn't just eat and drink in his room. He was also busy on the telephone to America. Because after spending only several evenings with Leslie, he had reached a decision.

The butler brought the telephone on a tray and held it toward Vanessa Prentiss. "Mr. Lance, madam. But I'm afraid you'll have to raise your voice a bit. It's a terrible connection."

As Vanessa's long fingers reached out to pick up the receiver, several large jeweled rings caught the light, momentarily dazzling the eye but doing little to conceal the liver spots that covered her bony hands. "Hello, my son," her deep voice rumbled through the static to Lance. "Have you dissipated more of the family fortune?"

She could barely hear him, but interspersed with the static she managed to grasp that he had rented a home in a place called Genoa City. He described the twenty-room house, saying that it was on a lake called Geneva. He thought the country would be good for her, and it would definitely be good for him, since the city was located smack in the middle of America. He said that he knew she was bored in Washington; the country would be a refreshing change.

Lance was surprised when she said, "All right, if it's something you want to try." He had expected a fight.

But Vanessa was a woman of unerring instinct. She had read between the lines, the static and the faulty logic. The damn fool boy had gone and fallen in love. Vanessa was perfectly willing to go to whatever province he had in mind, including Siberia. She was more than willing. Because only by being there could she put a stop to this idiocy. Right away. Before it grew.

Chapter Eight
The Housewarming

Laurie worked with a passion. Cigarette butts piled up in her ashtray. Coffee cups lined her desk. Her usually long, red, manicured fingernails got in her way, so she chopped them off in order to type faster. Her hair, normally a long heavy curtain swinging around her face, was caught up in a rubber band on top of her head.

She would show them all—Leslie, Brad, her parents, everyone in Genoa City and the world. She would show them all that she was someone to be reckoned with.

She was glad the whole ugly incident had happened with Brad, because her anger fired her work. Her novel had changed; it was no longer just the story of one woman's breakdown. Now it would include all of them.

She would show the world the real Leslie Brooks, expose her for the spineless worm she really was. Show how envy always motivated her, how selfish she was—always, always taking everything Laurie wanted. She would reveal how Leslie had always been her father's favorite—always, from the time they were little, and Laurie had been so outgoing, happy and playful. But her father had never noticed her, except to say, Laurie lower your voice; Laurie, why don't you behave the way your sister Leslie does, *she's* such a little lady; Laurie, hush now, your sister's practicing. It made her sick just to think about it.

But now the whole world would know the real Brooks family. And yes, Laurie had loved her mother, until that awful day when her mother had confessed that Laurie wasn't Stuart's daughter. How slimy, how seedy. But Laurie would write it all. She wished her mother had never slept with Bruce Henderson, because then she would never have been born. But since her mother had, Laurie wished she'd kept it to herself. Now, whenever Laurie was with Stuart, she felt uncomfortable. No wonder he'd never loved her.

And Brad. How he had used her! Even when they'd all first met, and she'd fallen head over heels in love with him, he'd never loved her, never, never, never the way he loved Leslie. But she would expose it all.

They had even taken the one joy from her life. For one shining moment someone had loved her. Yes, Mark had loved her for herself. But they had stolen even that from her because he wouldn't have her, knowing they were half brother and sister.

They had stolen everything from her, always. Awful, awful, awful. They'd never given her anything, not respect, not liking and certainly not love. Oh, yes, she would show them, show it all. And people would weep for the heroine of her book.

She just had to keep working hard like this, keep pushing. She would be finished soon.

Her book would be a grand success. It would make

Leslie's piano playing look like small potatoes. Nobody was interested in classical music, anyway, just a bunch of longhairs and jerks. But her book! Everyone would read her book. It would be on the *New York Times* bestseller list. She'd make a fortune, change her name and move out of this hole. Who wanted to be in Genoa City, anyway? Nothing interesting ever happened here.

The big house on the lake at the outskirts of Genoa City was ablaze with lights. The mile-long drive from the road to the house was lined with Cadillacs, Mercedes, Chryslers and several more-humble makes. Everyone who was anyone in Genoa City had been invited to Mr. Lance Prentiss's party.

In the past months, Lance had made the rounds of the offices of all the local important men. He'd stopped in to call on Stuart, explaining that Genoa City was perfectly located for his business. He'd had several tennis dates with Snapper and Greg, and his easygoing charm had won them over in no time.

Meanwhile, he'd had the house reconstructed to suit Vanessa's idiosyncratic specifications. He'd brought men in from Chicago to do the job perfectly —and to keep any local workmen from spreading gossip about the big house on the lake.

He'd seen Leslie, too, since their return from Mexico City, never having dinner with her more than once a week, never asking her anything personal, never offering anything personal about himself. Always the perfect gentleman—thoroughly discreet and utterly cautious. She never asked why he had chosen Genoa City; he never offered a reason. But every night as he lay in bed, he found himself imagining her at her piano, and he craved her with a passion that left him dazzled, unsure and yearning like a teenager.

After carefully paving the way for his introduction into Genoa City society by making contacts with the men in town, Lance sent out handwritten invitations to all the best families. On each he wrote that he would be honored if they attended a housewarming party, which he hoped would enable him to introduce himself properly to his neighbors.

All the ladies in town were in a snit about what to wear, pulling cocktail dresses from plastic cleaning bags and rejecting them. Telephones rang back and forth. Finally, Jennifer Brooks settled it for everyone: she said it was clear from his invitation that it wasn't a formal party. Once again, everyone dove into their walk-in closets, this time pulling out long velvet skirts and silk shirts or angora sweaters shot through with gold. But underneath all the discussions of appropriate dress, and the excitement of having a new, handsome, wealthy man in town, ran an undercurrent of interest and intrigue. Oh, yes, Stuart Brooks had said that Lance had said he'd chosen Genoa City for its location. But come now, a man like Lance Prentiss could fly anywhere he wanted—after all, he even had his own plane. By the evening of the party, anticipation ran high.

Laurie received her invitation, read it with raised eyebrows and tossed it on her hall table. She knew exactly why he was in town. She remembered quite well the evening of the benefit, how Lance had zeroed in on Leslie. Well, Laurie had no intention of going to his stupid party; she was too busy writing.

Several days before the party, Jennifer called to ask Laurie if she wanted a ride with the family. Laurie told her she wasn't going.

"But darling . . ." Jennifer's voice sounded shocked. "He's such an attractive man. And he's single, if you don't mind my being blunt."

"Mother, I'm busy."

"Busy doing what?"

"Mother, can't I ever, ever say anything without having to explain myself?"

"Laurie, please be a good girl. If you don't go, people will talk."

"Let them talk. That's all they ever do, anyway."

"Laurie, please? Do it for me."

"Oh, all right." Sometimes it was easier to give in than to argue. Besides, soon she would be free of Genoa City forever. She might as well go to the party. In fact, she had an idea—after she finished off this book about the Brooks family, she could write another one, all about Genoa City. It would make *Peyton Place* look like a comic book. She'd go to the party only to gather information.

Arriving an hour late, Laurie brought her Jaguar to a screeching halt in the gravel in front of Lance's house. She felt daring and reckless from the idea that soon she would be leaving Genoa City. One of the parking valets hired for the evening opened the car door for her. She got out and said with a big smile, "Put a scratch in this baby, and I'll break both your legs." The boy didn't know whether to laugh or not as he watched her long legs, glistening in black leather pants, stride up the front steps.

As she walked through the large white door into a grand entrance hall, pleasant conversation streamed from rooms on either side. Arbitrarily choosing the left door, she moved toward it, flipping her hair out from under the turned-up collar of her black leather jacket.

ONE SHINING MOMENT

She found herself in a large cathedral-ceilinged room that seemed like something out of a man's hunting lodge. A fire crackled in the huge fireplace, from which a large sheet of brass extended all the way to the high ceiling. People lounged on couches or stood chatting in small groups.

She scanned the room until she spotted her host, looking very handsome in an oversized brown sweater with a shawl collar thinly trimmed in red. He was smiling down into the eyes of a frowsy woman, holding her hand in both of his. The woman was blushing. Laurie wasn't sure who she was, but the dark print creation she wore looked like it had won the "ugliest dress of the year" award. Next to them, beaming benignly, stood an older, theatrical-looking man, resplendent in a burgundy velvet suit and white ascot. His leonine white hair was combed back in a magnificent pompadour, and he wore his pants high on his waist. Laurie didn't know who these people were, until she saw Leslie join their group and hand Lance a glass. Her keen eye discerned a certain familiarity between her sister and Lance. She realized the older lady must be Leslie's nursemaid, the man Leslie's coach.

Laurie moved toward the group and kissed her sister lightly on the cheek. "Hello, Leslie, you're looking very creamy and angelic this evening." She fingered Leslie's sweater. "Cashmere? And how nice to see you out and about with your little coterie." She nodded to the maestro and Miss Wakefield, both of whom looked mildly embarrassed.

Laurie held out her hand to Lance. "I don't think you remember me. I'm Laurie Brooks, Leslie's sister."

Lance took an immediate dislike to Laurie. He didn't like the tone of her voice, didn't like the way she'd seemed so contemptuous of Miss Wakefield, whom Lance had a soft spot for, and didn't like the way she'd been so cutting to Leslie.

He smiled his easy smile, but his eyes were hard as he shook her hand. "Did you leave your manners outside with your motorcycle gang?" he asked pleasantly. "I think I'm the one who should be introducing myself. Here, let me take that jacket, I beg you."

He helped Laurie off with her jacket and handed it to a passing waiter. "Will you please put this with the other coats? And at the end of the evening, check the pockets for silverware."

Leslie, Miss Wakefield and the maestro all looked embarrassed. And for a split second, Laurie was furious. But then she threw back her head and laughed heartily. She smiled at Lance, an odd little half smile, and said, "Welcome to Genoa City. It's about time we had somebody here who wasn't a namby-pamby. Where's the bar?"

Lance nodded in the bar's direction. She strode off, and Lance stood watching her leather-clad slim figure twitch away on high heels.

"Feisty little devil, your sister," he said to Leslie.

"I'm sorry, Lance. She's not always quite that obvious."

"You don't have to apologize to me. You two certainly don't seem to come from the same family, though," he said thoughtfully, still watching as Laurie cut her way through the crowd.

Lance found himself surrounded all night by friendly faces, being asked polite questions couched in terms that weren't too prying. He spent a good part of the evening with Stuart and several of the older men in the den, deep in conversation as they threw out little hints about the road spur that needed finishing in Genoa City. Lance, in turn, casually mentioned several well-connected friends who were often able to bypass bureaucracies to get things done. The brandies, cigars and handshakes pleased the men.

Lance played a few rounds of billiards with Snapper and Greg. He didn't promise anything more specific than dropping by the hospital to have a look around, but Snapper felt a fresh enthusiasm for his plans to expand the outpatient department. Greg was impressed with Lance's ability to understand sticky legal problems. They laughed and joked until Lance excused himself, saying he had to pay his respects to the ladies.

The ladies were interested in Lance's social aspects. Not one of them missed the fact that he seemed on very familiar terms with Miss Wakefield and the maestro, even though with Leslie he was nothing more than the picture of politeness.

Certainly he didn't try to hide their previous acquaintance. As he stood talking to Jennifer and several of the other ladies, he offered the information that they'd all run into one another in Mexico City —and that having seen Leslie again was one of the reasons he'd thought of settling in Genoa City. The ladies chewed this over at great length after he'd excused himself and moved on to another group.

Laurie, diligently applying herself to the acquisition of information for her next book, joined conversations that she usually avoided. She, too, pricked up her ears when she heard that Leslie and Lance had seen one another in Mexico City. Her eyes scanned the room, and sure enough, Lance and Leslie stood together in front of a curio cabinet in one corner of the room. Wishing she could hear what they were saying to each other, she watched from a distance as Lance reached up and took one of the little statues off the shelf and handed it to Leslie.

"I got this one when we were in Mexico," he said, trying not to put special emphasis on the words. "I've always been fascinated by various cultures' carvings of deities. This one is Quetzalcoatl, the Mayan god."

Leslie admired it, set it back on the shelf and asked what the others were.

For a moment, Lance couldn't answer. As she had reached up, her sweater had pulled tight against her breasts. Lance found himself yearning for her, wanting to touch her. He felt like a schoolboy, surprised that just a glimpse of swelling breast through a white sweater could arouse him more than all the revealing lingerie he'd seen on other women.

Leslie looked at him when he didn't answer right away. Suddenly, for the first time since she'd known him, she saw that look on his face, the look of hungry desire; and as she gazed into his blue eyes, she felt herself responding. She felt the coldness that had surrounded her for so long begin to thaw. Nervously, she looked away from him and excused herself, saying she was going to try some more of the wonderful food he'd provided.

Lance forced himself not to watch her walk away. Instead he turned to a woman who introduced herself as Kay, saying they hadn't had a chance to speak yet.

Laurie met Leslie halfway across the room and said smoothly, "Well, sister, town gossip has it that Lance was your constant escort in Mexico City."

Since their scene in the music room, Leslie had not spoken to Laurie, other than formalities. She felt that she had nothing to say to her sister now that she knew about her affair with Brad. However, at Laurie's direct question, Leslie replied that she had indeed had dinner on several occasions with Lance, that he seemed a gentleman and that there wasn't much more to it than that.

"Come off it, Leslie," Laurie snorted. "Don't give me that sweet voice and say there's nothing to it."

Leslie excused herself and walked toward the buffet table, but Laurie followed. "He's very attractive, Leslie. I wouldn't blame you if you fell for him."

Leslie stared at her coldly and said, "Laurie, you never understand anything I feel or do. Now kindly stop analyzing my actions and leave me alone." With that, she picked up a plate and began to make a selection from the coldcuts platter.

But Laurie stayed close to her sister and murmured into her ear, "Oh, I understand you all right, Leslie. I understand you want him. It's written all over your face. You always think you're so high and mighty, and that you have everything and everybody under control. Well, you don't. It's just a matter of time before you fall for him. If you haven't already."

Leslie found herself stabbing at the tray of meat with a fork as the telltale color surged to her cheeks. She wheeled away from her sister and carried her plate all the way across the room, to be as far away from Laurie as she could get. Her heart was pounding, and she felt feverish and flushed. She told herself that Laurie had no idea what she was talking about, but somewhere way in the back of her mind, a small voice whispered, *It's true, it's true. You do want him.*

Leslie, with Miss Wakefield and the maestro, left around midnight, pleading tiredness and saying she had to be up early to rehearse. Lance didn't try to keep her longer. And although he wanted to draw her toward him, wanted to bury his face in her sweater, wanted to lick her eyelids and cover her mouth with his, he was careful to shake her hand briefly and firmly and thank her for coming. But he had felt it, he thought with elation as he calmly closed the door and turned back to the party. He had felt it in her hand, felt the electricity spark between them, he had seen it in her eyes as she'd looked up at him for one brief moment before turning away quickly. His heart raced, and he went swiftly to the bar and threw down a shot of Wild Turkey. Yes, he had felt it. She wanted him, too.

By one, the last guests were piling into their cars. Laurie was among the very last to leave.

"Thank you." She held out her hand to him. "I hope you enjoy what you've come to find here in Genoa City. But I'd like to give you one little word of advice. She's not nearly as fragile as she looks." She tossed her hair behind her and tripped lightly down the steps to the driveway.

"Laurie," Lance called from the doorway, "be careful driving. You're on thin ice."

Her laugh echoed from the dark night as she made her way toward her car.

Lance was riled. Laurie had managed to leave a bad taste in his mouth at the end of a pleasant evening. He closed the door and began seeing to the business of overseeing the staff as they cleaned up.

Leslie only half listened on the way home as Miss Wakefield raved about Lance's home. What a simply masculine house it was, she exclaimed, with all that leather and brass, those Persian rugs and even the stag heads mounted in the den. She was particularly impressed by the two-foot-high band of smoked glass that completely rimmed the top of the walls throughout the entire downstairs. It was such a modern touch in a conservative house and showed such individual taste and style, didn't Leslie agree? When Leslie nodded absently, Miss Wakefield continued chattering away about how lovely the food had been, what an ample bar had been provided and how there had been just the proper amount of help—not so many that they seemed intrusive, but not too few to make things uncomfortable.

Leslie felt relieved when she could finally shut the door of the guest bedroom that she now used as her own. She got into bed and found herself thinking only of Lance. He hadn't talked to her as much as he might have; he had acted toward her as he had toward any number of other guests there. Except for that one moment.

In her mind's eye Leslie saw the expression on his face, the hunger that had been there for one brief moment. Her breath quickened, and she began to tingle. But she felt a mild embarrassment, too. These thoughts were wrong. How could she even let herself think such things?

Again, she told herself not to feel anything for anyone. It only led to confusion, made her lie in bed, tossing and turning, her equilibrium disturbed. She wanted only music. She didn't want this feeling—she didn't, she didn't, she didn't! But against her will, the image of his face came into her mind and made her feel flushed.

Lance sat in Vanessa's upstairs quarters sipping sherry. She had lit a fire in the fireplace, and only one dim light glowed. He had purposely turned his chair so that he faced away from the panels of glass that bordered the floor of her quarters. Over the years, he had grown accustomed to her insistence on being able to see whatever went on in the main part of the house without being seen. But tonight, with Leslie in his home for the first time, he had found himself cringing at the thought of his mother, ensconced in her big chair, staring down into the living room watching every move everyone made.

"Well, Lance, I knew it would happen sooner or later," said Vanessa. The filmy scarf she wore in front of her face moved a bit when she spoke. Lance hardly noticed it anymore; by now he was used to never seeing anything but his mother's eyes.

He looked nervously around the room, unable to meet her glance, feeling like a schoolboy caught with his hand in the cookie jar. Vanessa never missed a trick; her eyes must've been boring into Leslie all night. Oh, his poor, fragile Leslie, having to be inspected so coldly like that, as if she were a butterfly on a pin.

"But," Vanessa went on, "I certainly never expected it to be anyone who looked so much like a . . . like a . . . tart."

Lance looked at his mother, surprise on his face. "What are you talking about, Mother?"

"That hot little number in the black leather pants, who drank entirely too much and acted as if she didn't know you were in the room."

Lance was startled when he realized Vanessa meant Laurie. He opened his mouth to correct her, then shut it again. For once, his mother was wrong. Well, good, let her think it was Laurie he wanted. That would keep her off the track long enough for him to develop his relationship with Leslie.

Vanessa sat nodding, her filmy scarf fluttering

slightly. She knew her son, knew him well. He had fallen for a little devil.

They sat for a time in companionable silence. Vanessa felt sure that she could turn Lance's head from the little devil. And Lance, for once, felt safe from his mother's prying gaze.

Chapter Nine

Lovers At Last

Mr. Merrill shook Lance's hand heartily. "Pleasure doing business with you, Mr. Prentiss."

Lance smiled easily and said, "Why don't you call me Lance. I'm really just a regular guy who happened to be born loaded."

Mr. Merrill laughed with unfeigned mirth. "I like a man with a sense of humor. Call me Al. Now, don't worry. I'll follow your instructions to a T."

He didn't say out loud that his liquor store never did as much business in a year as the order Lance had just placed this afternoon. Lance had given him a typewritten list of the wines, spirits and fancy liqueurs he wanted, plus a system for automatically delivering certain bottles once a month. He gave him the names of wholesalers who had the sole rights for some of the imported stuff. And he handed Al a hundred dollars more than the bill total, saying he knew Al wasn't really set up to do business on this scale and the extra money was to cover long-distance phone calls plus whatever additional time this big order cost him.

As Lance left the store, Al repeated with heartfelt

honesty, "Pleasure doing business with you, Lance."
From behind his counter, he watched with interest
through the store window as he saw Lance look up
and smile easily. Then he saw Laurie approach from
the direction of the stationery store. As they began to
talk, Al smiled, shrugged and turned away to take
care of another customer.

"Ah, if it isn't the titan of industry," said Laurie,
smiling. Her red lips glistened in the cold afternoon
sun. "I really should've written to thank you for your
lovely party, but I've been busy writing other
things."

"Now I'm supposed to say, 'How fascinating. I
didn't know you were a writer.' Is that it?"

"Of course not. I wouldn't expect you to show any
interest in me. Not when you're so busy looking like
you're not interested in my sister."

"I thought your kind couldn't go out during the
day. That you had to wait for a full moon so your
fangs could grow to their proper length."

"Oh, no, everybody in town just holds crosses out
when they see me coming."

"Nice sunglasses."

Laurie pushed the black wraparound sunglasses
up on her nose. "You like them?"

"Yes, they cover up the daggers."

"Well, ta-ta. Pleasure talking to you. You're the
only one around this crummy town who knows how
to carry on a real conversation."

Laurie walked down the street, thinking that she
did kind of like Lance in a funny way. He really could
take what she gave out and hand it right back.

Lance felt riled. Everything about Laurie disturbed
him. He didn't like the tough way she dressed or
talked. He didn't like the feeling of dueling when he
spoke with her. He didn't like her at all, he thought

with distaste. Families were so amazing, how two sisters could be so totally different from one another. Brothers, too, he thought.

He moved down the street quickly. He had big plans this weekend.

Vanessa poured a cup of tea from the silver teapot and handed the cup to Lance. "So, you've laid the plans for the big seduction, and now you're packing Mother off to Washington, is that it?"

Lance sighed. "Actually, Mother, that's correct."

"I don't know why I have to go. I should think the tart would rather like the idea of someone watching. She strikes me as the kinky sort." Vanessa watched Lance's face carefully.

Lance was smug. His mother still thought it was Laurie he was after. "Frankly, Mother, she requested that we do it in your bed."

"Now, don't be fresh with me, young man. It's one thing for me to say wicked things. I'm an older lady. It's quite another for a son to be obscene to his mother."

"I'm sorry, Mother."

"You should be. But tell me, how does this girl know I'm here? I thought I was a deep, dark secret."

"She doesn't know. I was just teasing. No one in Genoa City knows you're here. And since no one knows, why don't you just be a doting mother and go away for the weekend. Please?"

"Tell me why you're not taking the minx off to a hotel. It seems so much more appropriate."

"Because, Mother, I don't want anyone to hear our wild animal screams."

"I asked you not to be fresh with me, Lance." She looked at him again. He was trying to seem easy and relaxed, but she knew he really wanted her to go. The little devil probably took drugs. Well, that was all right. Vanessa was beginning to feel more confident. If the devil was so forward and hopped into bed with Lance now, he'd forget about her that much quicker. Vanessa had seen many of them come and go, and goodness knew how many others she hadn't seen. Let him plan his little seduction. The sooner they did it, the sooner it would all be a thing of the past. Then she and Lance could leave Genoa City, although, Vanessa admitted to herself, she was growing fond of the lake, which she often watched from her quarters upstairs.

"All right, Lance," she said at last. "I'll go to Washington for the weekend. Just do me a favor."

"Yes, Mother?"

"Don't take anything addictive. It would be so trying to have to send you to one of those dreadful drying-out places for movie stars."

"You know me, Mother. I'll try anything—twice."

"That's what I'm afraid of. Aren't you even going to thank your mother properly for being so indulgent?"

Lance got up and moved toward her. Tenderly he said, looking into her eyes, "Thank you, Mother." He leaned over, kissed the top of her head and squeezed her shoulders.

He really did seem grateful. Vanessa hoped she was right in judging this to be nothing more than a silly infatuation.

"Oh, Lance, you shouldn't have!" Miss Wakefield gazed lovingly at the tiny figurine, a small bisque fox terrier, sitting on the coffee table in Leslie's living room.

Leslie smiled as she sipped a glass of white wine, sitting in one of the easy chairs. It pleased her that Lance was always so thoughtful of Miss Wakefield.

Lance sat in another chair, smiling fondly as Miss Wakefield picked up the dog. "But how ever did you know that I adore terriers?" she asked, her eyes shining.

"You happened to mention it once"—Lance shrugged—"and when I saw the dog, I thought, Miss Wakefield will love this."

"It's true. I do." She looked at him, blushing. "It really was considerate of you. I can't thank you enough." She turned the dog over and saw the markings on the bottom. "Oh, but Lance," she sputtered, "I'm really serious. You shouldn't have. This is a very valuable piece. I know my eighteenth-century English bisque."

"Yes, well, that's another thing you once mentioned. That's why when I saw this dog, I knew you had to have it."

Miss Wakefield shook her head. "Lance, please, I really can't accept such an extravagant gift."

"Miss Wakefield, money's only relative. I happen to be fortunate to have a lot of it. And I can't think of anyone in the world who would appreciate this piece as much as you. Please don't insult me and refuse it."

"It's true. I've never had anything I've liked so much in my whole life." Miss Wakefield was having trouble hiding the tremor in her voice.

"Well," Lance said, setting down his glass. "I suppose it's time we left. Leslie?" He tried as hard as he could to still his heart and maintain his light, easygoing manner.

Leslie looked up at him, her eyes wide with what almost looked like terror. She had thought about this date for days. Lance had called and asked if she'd like to have dinner, the way he had called so many times before, but even over the phone she could imagine that expression in his face, and she knew that it was in hers, too. Now that the night was here, she felt flustered. But she replied as coolly as she could, "Yes, I suppose it's time we left."

They all rose. Miss Wakefield chattered away happily, saying she was sure they'd have a wonderful time and to stay out late. Not to worry about her, there was a good mystery movie on the telly.

Lance helped Leslie on with her coat, and as his hands touched her shoulders, she felt her knees grow weak. They carefully avoided touching after that, just walked out of the door and down the path with Miss Wakefield calling good-bye merrily.

The night seemed refreshingly cool. The stars were out. They said nothing. Lance opened the car door; Leslie got in, and he walked around to his side.

She wanted to comment on the car, a 1956 Thunderbird in immaculate condition. She wanted to make small talk about how nice the car was, and how she'd never seen him drive it before: But she found that she couldn't open her mouth.

They drove in silence.

Lance felt Leslie's nearness in every fiber of his being. He felt her leg only inches from his, felt her shoulder close to his in the seat next to him. He wanted desperately to reach out and take one of her hands, lying folded in her lap.

Leslie felt his presence near her, could smell his after-shave lotion. There were always so many people around them. Although they'd driven to restaurants before, it had always been in bigger cars. It had never felt like this. In the small car, being alone seemed so intimate she could hardly stand it.

She still couldn't say anything when with pounding heart she saw him turn the car into the long gravel drive that led to his house on the lake. The sound of the tires crunched on the gravel. The mile seemed very long. Leslie's heart raced.

Lance pulled the car up in front of the house and turned off the motor. Suddenly it seemed intensely quiet. They sat listening to the silence, to an occasional birdcall, and to a pine cone as it fell to the ground.

He turned in his seat and faced her. She stared straight ahead, trying to control her emotions. Finally, she managed to say in almost a whisper, "I thought we were going to a restaurant."

His voice was husky. "Leslie, come into my home."

She couldn't answer.

He said, "We're always surrounded by people, always so formal. Leslie, please come into my home . . . and let your hair down."

Slowly she turned to face him, afraid that the longing inside her showed on her face. She managed to nod her head.

Lance got out of the car and came around to open her door. He held out his hand, and she took it. The burning feeling that shot from his hand up along her arm was so intense that she withdrew her hand from his.

They walked, side by side, not touching, up the steps and into the house. The entrance hall was dark, except for the warm glow of the fire that blazed in the hearth and spilled its light through the large double doors into the hall.

Neither of them could speak.

He took off his coat, his eyes never leaving her face, and flung it on a chair. He looked at her so longingly that she averted her gaze, afraid he'd see the same look on her face. Slowly she unbuttoned her coat but couldn't raise her head or take her coat off.

With sudden clarity, Lance realized that Leslie had never been with anyone but her husband. Lance was so used to being with worldly women that Leslie's shyness inflamed him even more. He had to be gentle with her, or she'd flee. He reached out and helped her off with her coat, whispering, "It's all right, Leslie."

His voice startled her, and she looked up at him with pleading eyes. He flung her coat next to his and, never taking his eyes from her face, reached up to take the pins from her hair. "I have wanted to do this for so long," he whispered huskily.

She felt her heavy locks fall around her shoulders. It was such a release, such a sudden feeling of freedom, that she put her head back and shook her hair.

"Oh, Leslie," Lance breathed, his voice thick. Gently he moved his face close to her neck. She could feel his breath. His lips felt soft as they grazed her neck and moved toward her ear.

She felt as if she could barely stand. Her body swayed and leaned against his.

"Leslie, I have wanted you for so long," he murmured in her ear. Slowly, tenderly, he unzipped the back of her dress.

The cold on her back was incredibly delicious, making her naked flesh tingle as his warm hands took her dress and slipped it from her shoulders. She had never felt so exposed in all her life. Never before had she allowed herself to be so vulnerable to a man. Lance was taking over her heart—her very soul. A low moan escaped her lips.

Then he was moving her into the living room,

somehow without her even knowing how, and her whole body felt alive with his touch, with the cold air and the sensuous feeling of nakedness. He lowered her onto the couch, and in the warm glow of the fire he whispered to her, touching her, telling her he had never seen a woman more beautiful, had never desired a woman so much, calling her his passionate angel. As he abandoned himself completely and began to make love to her, unable to hold himself back any longer, he mistook her sudden stiffening.

Brad bolted straight up, shouting, "Leslie!" He was sweating and confused. He told himself he was having a nightmare and lay back down on the rumpled sheets of his hotel room.

The fire had died down when Lance opened his eyes. His eyelashes brushed Leslie's shoulder. He felt her skin prickle with goose bumps and tried to cover her body with his. She felt so small under him. He raised his head to kiss her cheek and saw tears streaming down her face.

"Leslie, what's wrong?"

She couldn't answer. How could she tell him that she'd never made love with anyone but Brad, and that now she felt cheap? She felt humiliated. She wanted to cover herself, wanted to run, wanted to hide. But more than anything, she wanted Brad.

It had been exciting with Lance in the beginning, but there had come a point when Brad had entered her mind. Now she felt violated, debased at the realization that she had made love with anyone but him.

All she could say was, "Lance, would you please leave the room so I can dress?"

"But Leslie—"

ONE SHINING MOMENT

"Please, Lance."

"Of course."

He left the room, grabbing his clothes as he went.

As he quickly dressed in the hall, Lance realized that for Leslie this must have been a difficult move. But he knew he could make her trust him, if he just handled her as delicately as she required. She was like a little bird, a little dewdrop, a small, graceful piece of a rainbow. She was like the mountains, like the ocean, like a beautiful field on a spring day, with butterflies and birds and flowers—and with a deep rushing river coursing underground through a jagged riverbed of sparkling quartz and diamonds. She was everything. He hungered for her even more now, now that he knew he'd been right, that beneath her outward composure coursed a deep, almost violent passion. And he knew he was the man to release that passion—he had felt it in her response to him.

She appeared in the doorway of the living room, and he moved toward her, his arms outstretched. When she flinched, he dropped his arms to his side.

"I'd like to go home now," she said in a small voice.

"But Leslie, my love, it's early. We can go out and eat. I feel like I could eat a horse."

"Please, I'd like to go home."

Easy, big fellah, he told himself. She's very sensitive. Now, more than ever, is the time to go slowly, to be gentle with her.

"Of course, Leslie."

He helped her on with her coat, being careful not to allow his fingers to linger on her shoulders. They got back into the car, and he turned on the radio. Soft music played as he drove back to her house.

Before he had even pulled completely to a stop, Leslie had her door open.

"Leslie, wait!" Lance leaped out of his car, but by the time he caught up with her, she had run into the house and slammed the door.

The next morning Lance called, and Miss Wakefield answered, her voice quiet.

"Good morning, Miss Wakefield. Beautiful day." Lance's voice sounded happy. "Is Leslie practicing? Would you mind interrupting her?"

He heard Miss Wakefield's voice coming softly over the line. "No, Lance, she's in her room. I had a terrible time getting her to bed last night. Every time I tucked her in and went back to my room, she was up and at the piano again."

"I'll be right over," Lance said, and hung up before Miss Wakefield could tell him not to come.

"Send him away," Leslie said from behind her closed door.

Miss Wakefield fluttered outside the door. "Oh, but Leslie . . ."

"Send him away."

Miss Wakefield went slowly down the stairs. Lance stood in the hall, looking up the stairway expectantly. His face fell when he saw her. She drew her arm through his and ushered him into the living room. "I'm sorry, Lance," she said, worry showing on her plain face. "But you know, Leslie's rather sensitive. Things don't roll off her back like with other women. She *feels* so much, you know."

"But that's why I love her."

Miss Wakefield patted his arm. "I'll see what I can do. No promises, mind you. After all, I'm just hired help."

"You're more than hired help," said Lance.

Every day Lance called, and every day Miss Wakefield sounded more and more worried when she said that Leslie refused to speak to him. Every night, at strange hours, music came pouring out from the music room, filling the quiet night street with its plaintive sound.

Two weeks later, Lance knocked at the door. Miss Wakefield answered, and when she saw Lance, she shook her head sorrowfully. "Not today, either, I'm afraid."

But he pushed past her, and as he took the steps two at a time, he called over his shoulder, "Oh, yes, today."

Leslie heard his voice on the stairs. Throwing a robe around her and tying it tightly, she stood in the center of the small guestroom and waited for him. She could hear him calling her name, opening doors and shutting them until finally he burst through the door of the room where she stood.

He stopped for a moment, stunned. He had never seen her when she was really distraught, had never seen her wild hair or her ringed eyes. Swiftly he moved toward her and tried to take her in his arms.

She stood stock still, neither resisting nor embracing him, until finally he stepped back and looked at her. "You look like hell," he said.

She nodded. "Thank you. You don't look so wonderful yourself." Lance's face was drawn, and his clothes looked more rumpled than she'd ever seen them.

They stood, looking into each other's eyes, hers haughty, his searching. Finally he said in a soft voice, "Isn't this silly? You're not eating or sleeping. I'm not eating or sleeping. Why don't we stop this and eat and sleep together?" He gave a friendly little laugh.

He wasn't prepared when her hand darted out and slapped him hard across the face.

"Well . . ." He laughed, rubbing his face. "It could be worse. You could not care. Judging from that, I know you do."

"You're mistaken, Lance. I'm a married woman. I care only for my husband."

Lance took a step toward her, his voice suddenly lower. "Leslie, Leslie, I know you care for me. I felt it, I felt it when you opened your arms to me."

"I would prefer, Lance, that you have the decency never to mention that night to me again."

"Oh, no, Leslie," he said, moving toward her slowly. "I'll mention it again and again. The way you threw your hair back, the way you responded. I know, Leslie, I know what you felt. I felt it, too. You can pretend to yourself all you want, but you can't pretend to me. I was there. I felt you." He was standing very close to her.

She could smell his breath. She could see the rise and fall of his chest. She felt a longing begin inside her again for him. It was true: he had roused something in her. She didn't want to, but she felt it again.

"And you're feeling it now," Lance said, his eyes looking down into hers, his finger lightly tracing the satin V of her robe. "You're feeling it now, again. I can feel it. Something's happened between us, Leslie, something that nothing in the world can change. I can see it in your face."

She lowered her eyes and tried to calm the beating of her heart. "Lance, I'd like you to leave now."

"No, Leslie, I'll never leave you."

"I want you to leave."

"All right. I'll leave now." His hand touched her waist lightly and ran down her hip. He could feel her whole body tremble beneath her satin robe. "But I'll be back. Soon." He turned and walked out the door.

As he went down the stairs, he saw Miss Wakefield hovering nervously in the hall.

"I'll be back," he said over his shoulder, and slammed the door.

He called the next day and told Miss Wakefield to tell Leslie that he had to go away on business and would call when he got back. Let her stew in her own juices, he thought as he hung up the phone. He rambled around the big house with visions of Leslie tormenting him wherever he went.

He waited two more days, then went to Leslie's.

Miss Wakefield looked nervous.

"What's the matter," he asked, "hasn't she been sleeping?"

Miss Wakefield shook her head.

"I'll take care of that," he said. "Where is she?"

Miss Wakefield nodded in the direction of the music room.

Lance strode into the room. Leslie was standing at the piano, turning pages of music. She looked up when she heard his footsteps. "Oh, Lance," she said coolly.

Lance was taken aback. He'd been prepared to have her either throw herself in his arms or keep up the front a bit longer. He certainly wasn't prepared for the equilibrium she displayed.

"I'm glad you're here," she said.

"Good," he said, moving toward her, his body already yearning to touch hers.

But she walked away and stood on the other side of the piano, with her hands folded and resting on the piano top. "I thought about what you said."

"Good," he answered.

"And you were right," she said, still in the same cool voice.

"Of course I was, my darling," he said, starting to move around the piano toward her. But she held up her hand to stop him. "You did attract me. Strongly. But I'm afraid it's over. It was quite nice, but . . ." She shrugged.

"Nice?" Lance said incredulously. "You call one of the most . . . the most . . ." He searched for a word.

"Sublime?" she offered. "Passionate? Ecstatic?"

"Yes, all those things. You call what went on between us *nice*?"

"Yes, Lance. Nice. It was one of life's moments I'll savor when I remember it."

"Why are you talking about remembering it? It's only just begun," he said, moving toward her again.

She shook her head. "No, Lance. It's over."

"How can it be over?"

"Easily. Thank you so much for a lovely evening. I don't think I thanked you properly that night. I was a bit rattled. But now, I'd like to thank you before we say good-bye."

"Good-bye?"

"Yes, good-bye. I leave on tour again soon, and I need to throw myself into my work." She held out her hand to be shaken.

Instead he grabbed it and took her in his arms. He pressed her to him, but she stood still and unyielding. "Leslie, Leslie," he murmured in her ear.

"Lance, please." She drew away from him and moved toward the keyboard. "I really have a lot of work to do."

"You're talking about work when I'm talking about love?" he said, following her.

"This wasn't love, Lance; this was an infatuation." She sat down at the piano bench.

Lance stood staring at her. It was a pretty good act,

he thought, but it didn't fool him. If he could just rattle this calm she seemed to be wearing like a cape, he could get to her. He leaned against the piano. "I suppose you know all about love?" he said snidely, waiting to see her flush with anger.

"As a matter of fact, I do," she said, adjusting her music on its stand.

"And I suppose that you're talking about your husband?"

"Yes. I am."

Lance straightened and looked at her. "Well, if you have such a magnificent love, where is he?" he demanded.

"I don't know," Leslie said simply. "But that doesn't mean we don't love one another." For the first time, her voice took on warmth, and she looked at him kindly. "I'm sorry, Lance." She turned back to the piano.

"You're sorry? You're sorry? Is that all you have to say to me?" He felt anger mounting.

"Yes, Lance," she said, not looking at him. "That's all I have to say."

He stood for a moment. He wanted to shake her, wanted to rouse her from this calmness that had crept over her, wanted to grab her up and feel her arms around him. The silence grew.

Finally he said in a low, even voice, "Leslie, if I leave now, I'm never coming back."

"I think it's time for you to leave," she said, staring at the music on the rack before her.

As he left the room, Leslie held back. She began to play a light Mozart sonata so that he wouldn't know her true mood. But underneath, her heart was pounding, and she was fighting tears with everything she had. Because everything she had said had been true. It had been good with Lance, but she would never love anyone the way she loved Brad. And Brad had left her, for whatever reason he had. But she would never stop loving him.

And she would never love anyone else again.

Chapter Ten
Just One Of Those Things

Lance was beside himself with anger. He stormed down the path from Leslie's house and got into the car, then sat with his hands on the steering wheel, seething. He hadn't been this wildly angry since he was a teenager.

How did she manage to do this to him all the time? It was a loathsome feeling. He wished he'd never laid eyes on her. She had turned him into a frustrated, impotent teenage boy with more angry energy than he knew what to do with. There was only one way to vent this anger. Drive.

He looked at the steering wheel in his hands and shook it. This wasn't the car he wanted; this was one of the Detroit factory models he leased for everyday driving. No, right now he wanted a real car.

He drove to the lake, feeling his anger swell. He leaped out of the car, leaving the door open, and unlocked the side entrance to the garage he'd had built for his car collection.

His eyes scanned the dimness. Ah, there it was—his baby. He lowered himself into the deep leather seat. Already he felt better, his outstretched feet on the accelerator and clutch. He touched a button built specially into the high-tech dash and the garage door slowly slid open.

The long low black body of the Maserati emerged from the open door, its headlight covers closed. The entire sleek hood was one long black swath continuing along the small smoked windshield. The car took the gravel road in less than a minute, in first. At the head of the drive, Lance slowed. Easy, boy, just hang in until we're on the road, he thought, checking both ways and loving the perfect tension of the clutch as he eased it out.

The powerful motor surged, and the car leaped forward. He didn't need to check the dials; the whine of the motor told him the perfect moment to shift. He went faster and faster, luxuriating in the sound of the engine, the way the car hugged the road. Soon the leafless trees were nothing more than a blur as he took the car from one gear to another, downshifting and accelerating around curves, shifting back up again, flying faster and faster, away from his anger, away from Leslie, away from everything. There was nothing but Lance, his car and the empty, winding road. Free at last.

Laurie glanced down at the manila envelope lying on the seat next to her. Her pride. Her manuscript. It was finished. She was on her way to the post office to mail it to the New York publishers. Now it was just a question of time before she would be free at last.

She glanced at the rearview mirror. A black speck was approaching faster than anything she'd ever seen. Whatever it was, it must be doing at least 120, she thought. But before she had time to think another thought, or pull over, or do anything, the low black car had roared up behind her, pulled around her and sped off, leaving her behind as if she were standing still.

There was only one person in this town who could own a car like that, Laurie thought, raising her eyebrows. So, Lance was out taking a little joy ride, was he? But he didn't know the local roads as well as she did.

She could go to the post office in a while, she thought with excitement, and turned her car onto a back track she knew would cut several miles off the main road before intersecting it again.

Lance took another curve and squinted. Up ahead he thought he saw the red car he'd passed several miles back. And what was that? An arm pointed out of the driver's side. As his eye followed the hand, he saw some construction cutting through the wide-open fields. His mind moved fast: this must be the unfinished spur of the interstate Stuart had mentioned, he thought.

Lance saw the red car speed onto the spur. He smiled. So, some local hot-rodder wanted to race, did he? Good. He was in the mood for a race. But whatever the kid was driving couldn't possibly have the power of his Maserati, he thought, dropping down to fourth. He was close enough to see it now—Jaguar. If the kid knew how to drive, this could be a pretty good race, as long as Lance kept it down to fourth.

He pulled up alongside the car, both of them doing about sixty, then glanced over at the other driver, ready to give him a friendly high sign before the race started.

He did a double take.

Laurie smiled, saluted him and turned her face back to the road.

The last person in the world he wanted to see besides Leslie was her damn sister, Lance thought. He was just about to leave the spur in disgust when he had another thought. She wanted to race, did she? All right, he'd race her.

He held up one hand in a racing position and glanced over at her. She nodded with understanding. He counted to three, then lowered his hand.

And left her behind in thirty seconds.

Lance was leaning against the door of his car when Laurie pulled up to a screeching halt a few feet away. She turned off her engine, took out the keys and, throwing them up and down, walked toward him. "Pretty nifty toy you have there," she said, turning and leaning next to him.

"Take your weight off my car. You want to lean on something, lean on your own hunk of junk."

"Well, ex-cuuuse me," Laurie said, pushing herself off his car and going over and leaning on her own, opposite him. "Your daddy must be richer than mine."

"I don't have a daddy."

"Neither do I."

"What's that supposed to mean?"

"Nothing that you'd understand."

They stood in silence. There were empty fields around them, spotted with a few leafless trees. The day was cold and gray. Lance looked up and followed the flight of a circling bird with his eyes.

"I suppose," Laurie said, following his gaze, "that you're thinking something corny, like, Gee, I wish I was as free as that bird."

"As a matter of fact, I was."

"What's the matter, Lance? Genoa City suddenly turned boring?"

He shrugged.

"I told you so, I told you so," she said, but something about the look he shot her made her think maybe she was going too far.

"Well, *I'm* clearing out," she said.

"Oh, yeah? Am I supposed to ask where?"

She shrugged. "I don't know. Anywhere the spirit moves me."

"Maybe we'll be lucky and not run into each other."

"Why, are you going somewhere?"

Lance shrugged. "I thought maybe Europe. Winter's better there. Skiing. I don't know."

"I've never been to Europe in the winter," she said musingly.

"Is that supposed to be a hint?"

"Why in the hell would I want to go to Europe with you?"

"Why wouldn't you? Women are throwing themselves at my feet all over the world."

"Oh, yeah?" Laurie said, curling a lock of hair around her finger. "I don't see anybody throwing themselves at you around here."

Lance folded his arms across his chest and looked back up at the sky.

"What's the matter," Laurie asked, the cutting edge gone from her voice, "she throw you out?" She saw Lance stiffen and flash her another angry look. "Oh, come on, Lance. I watched the whole thing happen. You can tell me or not, you know. In a town this size, you can't flush the toilet without everybody knowing what you had for dinner."

"God, you're coarse."

"No, I'm not. I'm just honest."

They stood in silence again. Laurie opened her door, reached into her bag and pulled out a cigarette.

"Give me one of those," Lance said.

Laurie looked at him, surprised. "You don't smoke, do you?"

"There're a lot of things you don't know about me," he said, taking the cigarette. He grabbed the lighter out of her hand and lit her cigarette for her. "You have the manners of a fishmonger."

She cupped her hand around the flame and drew on her cigarette. "Aren't you sick of manners by now?" she asked.

"Manners are like money," he said, lighting his own. "You never get sick of either." He took a drag, pulled the cigarette out of his mouth and threw it down on the ground. "How can you smoke those things?"

She shrugged. "I don't know. I guess a lot of us do things we don't like and don't know why we do them—but can't stop."

"You can say that again," said Lance.

"I guess a lot of us do things," she said, laughing.

"Oh, shut up." He smiled.

"Uh-uh-uh." She wagged her finger at him. "Watch your manners."

He reached out and swatted at her hand. She pulled it away. "Well, your reflexes are pretty good," he said.

"You want to kick my tires and slam my doors?"

"Don't you ever quit?" he asked, laughing.

She shook her head. "Never."

"What's that thing sitting so importantly on the front seat?" Lance asked, nodding toward the manila envelope.

"Oh, that?" Laurie said casually. "That's my ticket out of here."

"Pretty fat ticket."

"Pretty fat book."

"Is it any good?"

"It's great," she answered.

"Oh, and modest, too." Lance laughed.

"I was on my way to mail it when I saw you. Now I just have to wait around kicking my heels and biding my time until the publisher accepts it. That's why I was thinking of going somewhere. Waiting around here gets very nerve-racking."

He looked at her. She stood leaning against her car, dragging on her cigarette and looking tough. But he had found as they'd been standing there that he didn't have to think, he just had to open his mouth and it didn't matter what came out. It felt so refreshing to him, so liberating, after the tortured months he'd spent censoring every word, worrying, going slow, being careful. Suddenly he felt exhilarated. All the anger was gone. Well, maybe that wasn't true —but it wasn't the burning anger he'd felt before. The car ride had washed most of it out. And standing here talking to wise cracking Laurie had relaxed some of the tension, made him feel free from the weight he'd been carrying for so long.

"You know what, Laurie? I'm serious. You want to blow this firetrap?"

She looked at him. He really was serious. "Twist my arm," she said, laughing.

"I've got my own plane," he coaxed.

"Bully bully for you," she replied, looking at her fingernails.

"I could give you a lift to Europe. And then we could go our separate ways."

"Now that's not a half-bad idea."

"Oh, come on. Why not? Give them all something else to talk about."

Laurie stiffened. "Sorry, chump. You're not using me to get back at her. I've already run that route."

"What do you mean?"

"It's a long, boring story."

"You can tell it to me on the plane. It's a long, boring ride."

Laurie shook her finger at him. "You're not getting me to tell you anything. I'm so sick of gossip I could puke."

"You're right. We'll make some ground rules."

"Uh-oh. Forget it," Laurie said, throwing down her cigarette and stamping on it. "I'm sick of rules, too. I just want to go where I can be free."

"Wait a minute. There's just one." He looked her in the eye. "You don't ask any questions, I don't ask any questions." He couldn't mention Leslie's name. But Laurie knew what he meant.

"With great pleasure," she said, bowing dramatically. "When do we leave?"

"How soon can you pack?"

"What do I need?"

"Nothing. I'm a very rich man."

"Forget that stuff, buddy. What do I need?"

"You need a toothbrush, a warm coat, an evening gown and a pair of dungarees."

"A lot you know about women. I can be ready in an hour."

"That's too soon. I've got to take care of a couple of things." He sounded preoccupied. "How about tomorrow?"

"I guess it takes titans of business longer than writers to clear the decks."

"Shut up," he said. "I'm thinking." He glanced at

his watch. Suddenly he felt as if he couldn't get out of Genoa City fast enough. "The plane's hangared in Chicago. You be at my place at two tomorrow. You can leave your heap in my garage. We'll drive to Chicago in this baby." He was already in his car, the engine roaring.

"You afraid if you pick me up, people will see you and talk?" Laurie called to him.

"Who cares?" he hollered back. "That's all they do anyway."

"You're okay," Laurie yelled after him. "Whoooeee!" She was thrilled. She would mail her book, pack and get out of here. If she got sick of Lance in Europe, she'd take off by herself. Free at last!

Lance didn't even bother driving back to the house; he headed straight for the turnpike. At the first rest stop he hopped out, ran to a pay phone, pulled out his credit card and gave the operator a Chicago number.

"Hank? Is that you?" he yelled above the *whoosh* of traffic.

"Sure it's me," answered Hank in his laconic cowboy drawl.

"I'm on my way in. Anything wrong with the plane?"

"'Course not. You pay me enough to keep it runnin'."

"You're not kidding. I should be there"—Lance checked his watch—"in, say, an hour, hour and a half. I want to go to Washington tonight, then come back to Chicago, and tomorrow night we're heading out to Europe."

"Roger, over and out."

Lance placed another call, to Washington, leaped back in his car, leaped back out, ran into the restaurant, drummed his fingers while they filled a coffee cup, threw a handful of money on the counter, ran back out and sped away.

Vanessa jabbed at some flowers and then wheeled from the vase. "Really, Lance," she said, her eyes flashing with anger. "This has gone on long enough. First you hustle me off to Washington, saying it's for a weekend. Then I get wild, mournful calls from you every day, begging me to stay away. Then you show up here looking like something the cat dragged in and tell me you've come to say good-bye before you fly off to Europe. I demand an explanation."

"The explanation is simple, Mother. I'm bored in that little town."

"Oh, you're bored, are you? I don't know anything about this young lady—and I use the words loosely —other than that she dresses in very bad taste. But I should say from your behavior that she's anything but boring."

Lance's head snapped up. Vanessa was still talking about Laurie. She didn't know anything about Leslie.

"Mother, it's nothing like what you think."

"It's never anything like what a mother thinks, is it, Lance? Now suppose you tell me exactly what is going on."

"I told you. Nothing is going on. I'm bored with Genoa City, that's all. I'm going to take a vacation."

"If I don't get some answers, I'm going to make your vacation a very frugal one."

"Mother, please stop threatening me with money. You know as well as I that I've managed to turn my trust into a fortune in its own right."

"I can't imagine how. You never seem to do any work."

"I don't have to. I hire all the best people."

"Well, at least your business people are the best. I can't say as much about the company you keep."

"Mother," Lance said, walking toward her, "are you going to say good-bye to me nicely, or are we going to have long, tearful phone calls from Europe?"

Vanessa walked back to the vase and began fiddling with the flowers. "When are you leaving?" she asked.

"Tomorrow."

Vanessa turned, trying to smile. "Well, good. Then we can spend a nice evening together here before you leave."

Lance looked at her guardedly, then blurted out, "I can't. I'm going back to Chicago tonight, and then leaving from there."

Now why, thought Vanessa, would he go back west? "Why?" she asked, her eyes flashing again. "Is the little tart back in Genoa City packing underwear from Frederick's of Hollywood?"

"Mother, it is really not what you think at all."

Vanessa snorted. "In that case, if it's not too much to ask of you, I'd like to be flown back to Genoa City."

"Why?" Lance asked, surprised.

"To tell the truth," Vanessa said, "I've grown an attachment to that lake. I'm even thinking of stocking it."

"Yes, but you'll be there all alone."

"That never seems to bother you when you don't want me around. But don't worry about me, Lance. I have my staff."

Vanessa held the curtain aside a crack and stood staring onto the driveway below. She knew Lance was furious with her. Because she and her staff had

joined him, it meant that instead of flying back to
Chicago, they'd had to fly straight to Genoa City's
small airport. She had promised to hire the finest
driver to get his Maserati back to Genoa City from
Chicago.

She watched as Lance paced back and forth in front
of the house, checking his watch and looking down
the drive. She watched Hank leaning against a tree
with a piece of grass in his mouth. She watched as a
red Jaguar pulled up and the tart jumped out, smiling.

She saw Lance point to his watch, saw the tart
shrug and laugh, saw Lance grab her arm and wheel
her toward one of the leased cars, her hair swinging
out in a wide arc. She saw Lance push the tart into
the backseat and slam the door, walk back to the
Jaguar, drive it into the garage and come out carrying
two bags. He threw them into the backseat, got into
the passenger side and signaled for Hank to drive
away.

Vanessa had hoped he might look up and wave.
But he didn't.

She knew she shouldn't have allowed herself to be
sent away. Those two were deeply in love. And from
what she could tell, neither of them knew it yet.

But there was still time, still things she could do,
she thought, slowly letting the curtain fall down and
cover the window again.

Lance and Laurie sat side by side in a crowded
London pub. The room was noisy and smoky. Each
of them raised a quart of ale.

"Oh, I say," said Lance, pushing his front teeth
over his bottom lip.

"Pip-pip," Laurie said, doing the same.

"Cheerio."

"Down the hatch."

"Hail Britannia!"

They clicked their mugs and drained them, sputtering and laughing.

"You know, Lance," Laurie said in a "veddy British" accent, wiping the foam from her lip. "We've seen the changing of the guard, the Tower of London, and Piccadilly Circus."

Lance nodded. "Yes, I know, matey," he answered in the same thick accent. "And we've danced in every private club in London, and seen Albert Hall, and annoyed bobbies, and driven on the wrong side of the road to I don't know how many cold castles, and eaten fish and chips 'til they're coming out of our ears." He leaned forward across the table. "How about you, Hank," he whispered a bit tipsily. "Had enough of these Bucky beavers?"

Hank shrugged, amusement crinkling his eyes. "You're the boss."

"Oh, *I'm* the boss." Lance feigned shock. "I thought *you* were the boss. Imagine that. Well, if I'm the boss, then I guess I can leave any time I damn well please, can't I? How long do you need to do tiresome things like get flight clearance?"

Hank pulled the wooden matchstick he'd been chewing out of his mouth. "I guess we can take off tomorrow, barrin' any unforeseen terrorist acts."

"Splendid!" Lance smacked his hand on the table. "Now then, where shall we go?" He looked at Laurie.

"Wherever," she said.

"What country is wherever in?" Lance asked.

"I don't know. I've never been there."

Lance thought for a moment. "You know," he whispered, drawing all their heads together, "I'm a bit sick of all this stiff-upper-lip stuff. Why don't we go somewhere where the people are warm and friendly. And where they know how to drink."

"Oh, come on, Hank," Laurie said, drawing her arm through his. "Don't be such a stick-in-the-mud."

The three of them were strolling along, Laurie in the middle, through the Piazza San Marco in Venice at twilight. Great flocks of pigeons rose up, swooped around the high tower and settled back in the piazza, where people threw out handfuls of grain. Tall black lamps with pink globes twinkled in the lavender twilight. All around the sides of the piazza under long arcades, store windows displayed a dazzling array of jewels, lace and crystal.

"It's incredibly beautiful here," said Laurie.

"It certainly is," Lance answered.

They continued to walk.

"Which do you think is more beautiful?" Laurie asked, looking at the magnificent cathedral in front of them. "This piazza or those Spanish steps in Rome?"

"I thought we settled the boring beauty question two weeks ago when we went to Paris and strolled down the Champs-Élysées. You were raving about that."

"I don't know," said Laurie, "I liked those little islands in Greece."

"That's just because you were the only woman within a two-hundred-mile radius who weighed less than four-hundred pounds and had any teeth."

"Get out of here!" Laurie laughed and steered them toward the great expanse of water that was the Grand Canal. "I think, after seeing all the places we've seen, I'm glad we're back in Italy. I think it's my very favorite country," she said, looking out at the great gold dome of the church that sparkled in the twilight across the Grand Canal. Small gondolas and larger boats rocked gently against the piers. Seagulls cried out from buoys in the water.

"Ho-hum," Lance yawned. "How pedestrian. Everybody always likes Italy best."

Laurie spotted an ice-cream shop at the corner of the grand piazza. "I'm hungry," she said, beginning to drag them toward it.

"How can you be hungry?" Lance laughed, pulling back on her arm. "We just finished a huge meal."

"All right." Laurie stopped dead in her tracks. "I'm not hungry."

"Well, which is it? Are you hungry or not?"

"What difference does it make?" Laurie said petulantly. "These people torture you. First they make you eat breakfast standing up. Then they make you hurry up and finish shopping so you can go out and eat a great big meal that you didn't want in the first place. Then they make you wait around until you're really starving before they'll open their kitchens. Then, late at night, they stuff you and get you drunk as a skunk. And the whole time, they're smiling and laughing like they know something you don't. You know why they're laughing? Because we're all so fat. I must've put on ten pounds in the last week alone. I can't even zip up my pants."

"Speaking of breakfast," Lance said musingly.

"I finished speaking of breakfast."

"Tough. Speaking of breakfast, remember hotcakes?"

"Oh, boy, do I. Remember bacon and eggs?"

"Remember Rice Krispies?" Lance said longingly.

They walked in silence for another moment.

"Hank?" said Lance.

"Probably tomorrow. Barrin' any unforeseen terrorist acts."

Lance was at the counter converting all his European money to American dollars. Hank and Laurie stood by their bags a few feet away.

"You know somethin', Laurie?" said Hank. "I've never seen Lance this way with a woman before."

Laurie looked at him. Hank had spent the whole trip with them, going everywhere they went. Each of them had had their own room, usually on the same floor, and they had all said good night at the same time. They had eaten together, laughed together, gotten drunk together and been hung over together. But this was the first time Hank had said anything directly to Laurie.

"I'm not a 'woman' with Lance, Hank. We're just friends."

"Uh-huh," Hank nodded.

"We are," Laurie repeated.

"Well, you just keep playing hard to get like this, and you'll have him before long."

"I'm not playing hard to get. We don't want each other. This is fine just the way it is."

Hank nodded. "Uh-huh," he said, and picked up the bags as Lance joined them.

Laurie woke early and stretched. She got up, went to the window and looked down on a beautiful sunny day in New York. Lance had suggested the Algonquin Hotel in honor of the appointment Laurie had made with the New York publishers.

She was excited; her appointment was for today. She looked at her watch: it was 8 A.M. They'd been out dancing until 2. But she was excited.

She put on her robe, slipped out of her room and tried the door to Lance's room. It was locked.

She looked around the hall and saw a maid's cart filled with clean towels standing in the hall. Padding back to her room, she grabbed some money and went out into the hall again. The maid refused. "Come on," said Laurie. "He's my boyfriend." She gave the maid a tip and was soon tiptoeing up to Lance's bed.

"Get up," she said, staring down at him.

He opened one eye, saw her, pulled the pillow over his head and said, "Get out."

"Get up," she said louder.

"Get out," he repeated louder, his voice muffled under the pillow.

She leaned over and pulled the pillow away from his face. He was laughing. "Get up!" she said, standing with her hands on her hips, smiling down at him.

Suddenly his smile changed. "Come here." He crooked a finger at her.

She backed away, shaking her head. "Oh, no, you don't."

He sat up in bed, scratching his head. "Why not? I can't believe I never thought of it before this."

"Oh, so you never thought of it before, huh?"

"Well . . . " Lance pursed his lips. "Maybe it did go through my head once or twice. We've done a lot of drinking."

"Buzz off," she said, leaving the room laughing, but quickly.

Lance flopped back in bed smiling. Now that he thought of it, it wasn't such a bad idea. They had an awful lot of fun together. She was easy to be with. They laughed a lot. He didn't feel any of the constraint he had with . . . His mind drifted back to

Leslie. He certainly didn't yearn for Laurie the way he had Leslie. That yearning was almost gone. In fact, he hadn't even thought of her for weeks, to be honest. He'd been feeling too good to even bother thinking about all that.

Lance lay in bed thinking.

Snapper sat in Stuart's office. He knew Brad had insisted that Leslie not be told. But he felt it was wrong that no one knew. He took a deep breath.

"There's something that I think you ought to know, Stuart," he said.

Chapter Eleven

A Friendly Hug

Vanessa drew her Persian lamb coat tightly around her and raised her face to the wind. The feeling of the breeze on her unexposed face was glorious. For so many years she had only felt the filmy presence of her scarf or the stuffy indoor air when she unveiled in her quarters at night.

In an odd way, for all the wrong motivations, Lance had been right to take this property, she thought. It was large and private. Large enough for her to walk far from the house, far from the curious eyes of the staff, all of whom had served her for many years. Large enough for her to come out here to the lake, where she could luxuriate in the freedom from her scarves.

Her eyes scanned the wide lake, gray, calm and wintry, surrounded by a thick forest of evergreens. A few ducks bobbed and honked on the surface. They seemed to be adjusting as well as she was to their new home. Vanessa had made a few phone calls and been told which ducks would suit this particular climate. She had even named them—stupid names, she realized, but even stupidity seemed a great release to her. She had ignored the genders of the three pairs. She smiled as Donald, Daisy, Huey, Dewey and Louie, and Uncle Scrooge paddled along, dipping into the water, coming up, shaking their heads and honking at one another.

Vanessa's hand felt for the postcard she had stuffed into her pocket on the way to the lake. She drew it out and looked at the picture. The Piazza San Marco in Venice. Turning it over, she read Lance's firm, clear handwriting:

"Glad you're not here. Only kidding. Think of you constantly. Have picked up several goodies that will make your beady eyes light up. Some of the goodies I've picked up are none of your beeswax. Will be home when I'm home. Your loving son, Lance—that is, not Lucas. (Just thought I better add my name so you knew who I was.)"

Vanessa shoved the postcard back in her pocket and began to walk slowly along the lake's edge. Lance was always reminding her of the difference between him and his brother. As if she needed to be reminded. She shrugged. It was normal, she supposed. She had tried her best not to make Lance feel guilty. But after all, wasn't he the reason she spent her life like a prisoner?

She tried to push the memories out of her mind, but they rushed over her again, unbidden. She remembered how the sunlight had been streaming in through the window where she'd stood arranging a vase of roses from the garden. The smell that had suddenly reached her nostrils and made her adrenaline flow. The smell of smoke. She'd dashed out of the morning room and into the hall. Smoke crept down the stairs. Leaping up the stairs, she'd seen Lucas, poor little child, his eyes wide with terror, hugging the wall, while smoke had billowed out from the boys' bedroom.

She'd dashed to the doorway, but the smoke had driven her back. Flames leaped everywhere. She'd shouted to Lucas, "Where's Lance?" His little lips had trembled. She'd looked with horror, and through the smoke, on the far side of the room, she'd seen her son, *her son*, the flames leaping tall, separating her from him.

She'd shot through the flames, not feeling anything, anything but the desperate need to get to her son. Grabbing a blanket from the bed, she'd wrapped it around him and, still feeling nothing, had swept him up and run back through the flames.

The memories became more fragmented after that. Memories of the servants' voices shouting. Hazy memories, of an ambulance, a hospital. Waking, crying out, "My son!" Feeling gentle hands ease her back down, hearing gentle voices say, "He's fine." Then she'd slipped back into a painful semiconsciousness.

Memories of the fire marshal sitting by the side of her hospital bed, nervously twisting his hat, saying that they had found certain evidence . . . hesitating, looking at her with pleading eyes, stumbling, mumbling, finally getting out the words that it appeared the boys had been playing with matches.

Memories of watching her two boys' frightened faces. Frightened from her bandages, and the hospital. Trying to draw them close to her, one by one. Trying, through the horrible bandages, to ask what had happened. Finally saying she knew they'd been playing with matches, they didn't have to pretend.

Memories of Lucas, the little one, saying in his baby's voice, "No, Mommy, I wasn't playing with matches. You said never to." And Lance, a bit older, looking at his brother with an odd expression for a child so young. Vanessa had been able to see it even through her pain and bandages. It had been the expression of an old, wise man on a little boy's face.

She'd watched her son square his little shoulders, her heart almost breaking at his gesture, as he'd looked her in the eye and said, "It's true, Mother." Her heart had filled with pride for her son, who was honest enough to admit the horrible thing he'd done. She'd held out her arms to draw him close, to hold him, to keep him close to her always, the way she did even now, after all these years, the fire, saving his life—and his honesty keeping them tightly bound to one another forever.

Mr. Deever slipped his half glasses off his nose, folded them and placed them carefully on his desk. He studied Stuart for a moment, liking the way Stuart sat calmly on the chair across from him. He liked the way Stuart had been clear and succinct, telling Mr. Deever that he knew Brad had gone blind, and that he had come to see Mr. Deever because his name had been listed as attorney on the application for a formal separation filed in the county court. Stuart's voice had faltered only once, when he'd mentioned that his daughter wasn't well. Mr. Deever was used to reading between the dry lines of legal jargon and deducing the emotional content hidden therein. He understood from Stuart's manner and choice of words that the poor woman must be suffering greatly. But Mr. Deever had his duties.

"I appreciate your concern, Mr. Brooks. But Mr. Elliot has left very clear instructions. Under no circumstances am I to disclose his whereabouts to anyone."

"But Mr. Deever," Stuart said, real pain showing in his face, "my little girl's heart is breaking."

Mr. Deever let his stiff manner slide a bit. He said with sympathy, "My jurisdiction is far from matters of the heart. But I can tell you this: Mr. Elliot has been more than liberal in the terms of the divorce."

"Divorce!"

Mr. Deever nodded. "I advised him that with the laws what they are now, he was being foolish. He insisted on liquidating only a fraction of his assets for his own use. He was adamant—against my better judgment, mind you—that the bulk of his holdings be placed in your daughter's name."

Stuart's voice was tight. "What are the grounds for the"—he hated the word—"divorce?"

"Incompatibility. It's quite standard now."

"Incompatibility? Those two were made for each other."

Mr. Deever shrugged. "If it's any consolation to you, it would appear from the terms he's specified that he's still deeply in love with your daughter. All I can tell you is that your son-in-law is a very strong-willed, principled young man. Stubborn," Mr. Deever added, for the first time showing the human being behind the lawyer's façade, "but highly principled."

Vanessa strolled back to the house. Her memories had disturbed her so much that she had walked briskly for miles, her head slightly lifted, the cold air caressing her face, until she'd begun to feel her usual calm return. Now she felt better—better, in fact, than she'd felt in years. She slipped her scarf back on.

As she approached the back of the house, she could hear her servants laughing in the kitchen. She glanced at her watch; it was their lunchtime.

Quickly she strode around to the front of the house. Her house, she thought triumphantly, and pulled the scarf off her face. She let herself in the front door, although quietly, not wanting the servants to hear her. She went into the living room and walked around it; how free her face felt! Dropping the filmy scarf on the arm of the couch, feeling scandalously daring, she allowed herself one more moment of freedom in the main part of the house before she went up the stairs to her quarters.

Lance opened the front door, placed his bag down, gestured for Hank and Laurie to follow and bellowed into the quiet house, "Anybody home in this mausoleum?"

He went into the living room and began turning on lights and throwing back the blinds, saying, "Come on in. Make yourselves at home."

James appeared from the back of the house. "Welcome home, sir," he said, allowing himself a small smile.

"Ah, James, how's it hanging?" James pursed his lips smilingly. "Can you rustle up some grub for three tired, hungry travelers?"

"Certainly, sir."

"But, James, nothing foreign. We want the best homemade American breakfast you can make."

"Certainly, sir."

Lance knelt and built a fire, then stood up, rubbed his hands together and smiled. "Ah, home. I'll be right back." He looked at the two of them standing in the middle of the big room. "I'm serious. Get comfortable. There's a stereo in the den. Go put something on, something loud. Get a little life around here," he told them as he ran up the stairs.

He knocked on Vanessa's door and then poked his head in. "Guess who's home," he called.

"The bogey man," said Vanessa, and Lance went into the room, closing the door behind him. They embraced.

She held him at arm's length, smiling. "Now, let me look at you." She patted his stomach, eyebrows raised. "Ah, ate your way through Europe, did you?"

Lance laughed.

"I've got a bunch of stuff for you down in the car," he said.

"Bananas grow in bunches."

"Right. I'll bring your bananas up later. I've got some company downstairs, but I just wanted to come up and say hello."

"It's quite all right. I haven't seen you in over a month. A few more hours won't matter."

Lance stopped and looked at her. Her hair was less formal than it usually was. She seemed looser, somehow, less stiff. "Mother, you look terrific."

"Thank you," she said, her eyes shining. "I've been having a perfectly marvelous time going outside. But run along. I can tell you all about it when we can really talk."

He kissed her on the cheek, looked at her and said, "I really am glad to see you."

She waved him out of the room and sat down in her chair. From there, she could see the little devil. Vanessa sighed. She had hoped that Lance would've tired of the tart by now. She couldn't stand the way the little devil sat there, her legs crossed on the coffee table, her arms and hair draped up over the back of the couch. The girl displayed an appalling lack of upbringing.

Vanessa wasn't too thrilled about the fact that

Lance's pilot also sat in the same position on the opposite end of the couch. She wished Lance weren't so democratic; he never understood that you shouldn't socialize with people who work for you.

She watched as Lance entered the living room, smiling and talking easily, and held her breath, waiting to see some romantic sign, something that would make her cringe. Instead, all she saw was Lance draw up a big easy chair, nearer to Hank than to the devil. He kicked his shoes off and brushed Hank's legs aside so he could stick his feet up on the coffee table, too. Really, Lance, thought Vanessa, you are much too informal with hired help.

But as she watched, she couldn't detect one sign of anything going on between Lance and the devil other than camaraderie. Could it be possible? Could the devil be so skillful that they hadn't yet consummated this relationship? Vanessa was very, very worried.

Then Vanessa saw the girl's long red fingernails pick up the scarf from the couch arm. Oh, dear, thought Vanessa. She'd forgotten about that.

Teasingly the girl held it aloft and swung it. Vanessa saw her point to the monogram and raise her eyebrows. Her red mouth formed the letter *V*. Then she said something that made Hank laugh. She saw Lance say something and lean forward to grab the scarf. Pulling the scarf away from his reach and swinging it, the girl said something else that made her throw back her head and laugh. She wagged her finger at Lance, who shook his head. Vanessa realized that Lance hadn't mentioned her to the devil. That was one good sign; at least they weren't talking too much. No real intimacy had been established, she thought, beginning to feel a bit better.

Then she saw all three heads turn as they rose, the girl carelessly dropping the scarf where she'd found it. Now the devil and the pilot were probably going to eat her out of house and home, she thought as she watched them leave the living room.

But she was feeling a bit better. She still had time. . . .

Lance rubbed his hands together as James brought in platter after platter of breakfast food. "Dig in," he said to Laurie and Hank, both of whom were a bit awed by the butler.

"Will that be all, sir?" asked James.

Lance answered with his mouth full as he stood up and reached across the table to grab a muffin. "Sure, it's great. Thanks. I'll holler if we need anything."

James withdrew.

Lance looked up just as he was about to stuff a forkful of scrambled eggs into his mouth. "What's the matter with you two? Dig in."

Laurie put her napkin in her lap. "It's all rather la-di-da, the way you live, Lance."

Lance shrugged. "You get used to it. Wasn't it you I had that conversation with?"

"Which conversation?"

"The two things you never get tired of."

"Yes, it was me."

They looked at each other across the table. That conversation seemed so long ago. But they had both been feeling slightly hostile toward one another then. And now they felt . . . What did they feel? Nervously they looked at their plates.

Hank's crinkled eyes took in the look that was exchanged between them. It was sure taking them long enough, he thought, reaching for the bacon.

They all stood in the hallway, feeling slightly awkward. They'd spent so much time together that it felt funny to be saying good-bye, and no one knew how to do it.

James appeared. "Your room is ready whenever you'd like it," he said to Hank, faintly allowing his displeasure to show over Lance's insistence that Hank have a room in the main part of the house.

Hank picked up his bag and said, "Well, good night."

Laurie looked at him. "That's it? Just like that? Good night?" She reached up and swiftly gave him a big bear hug. "You're a lot of fun, Hank, even if you hardly ever open your mouth."

He hugged her back. "You're okay yourself," he said. He walked up the stairs, leaving Lance and Laurie alone.

She reached into her bag, fumbling for a cigarette.

"Oh, come on. You don't need one of those," Lance said, grabbing her hand.

She pulled it back. "How do you know what I need?"

"You want me to answer that?" he said, smiling down into her eyes.

"No," she said. "I don't. I'll tell you what I need. I need to go home and get cracking on the list of things the editor said to do."

"Do you think you can do it?" he asked.

"Oh, sure," she said confidently, her voice not betraying the nervousness she felt. "And you? What are you going to be up to?"

"I suppose I should attend to some business."

"Yes, you are a businessman, aren't you?"

"In a manner of speaking," he said.

Again they stood in silence. Finally Laurie said, "Well, it's been real."

"Yes, it has," Lance said, and meant it.

She slugged him on the shoulder. "Okay, this is growing into the long good-bye. Give me a call sometime. My number's in the book." She reached for the doorknob.

"Aren't you even going to hug me? You hugged Hank."

She turned and faced him. "But that was different."

"I know. We're different men."

She shook her head.

"How about a little peck on the cheek?" he said, laughing and pointing to his cheek.

She laughed, too. "Nope. Nothing doing."

He leaned against the door, stopping her from leaving. "I think you're right. It's probably better this way."

"I know I'm right," she said, trying to push him out of the way. But he stood there, blocking her exit.

"Laurie, calm down for a minute." He was still smiling. "I want to tell you something. All kidding aside"—he put his hands on her shoulders—"I have really never, ever, *ever*, had as much fun as I've had with you this past month."

"I bet you say that to all the girls," Laurie said, nervous from the serious tone in his voice.

"No, I don't. I tell them I adore them, I'm crazy about them, I long for them, I have to have them." He laughed as she hit him in the arm. "I never tell anybody anything that isn't true. And this is true. I've never had so much fun."

She looked down, then up at him. "Me either."

And it just seemed so natural. They slipped into each other's arms and hugged, swaying back and forth, slowly. "You feel good," he said in her ear.

"So do you," she answered.

"Thank you so much for a wonderful trip," he said.

"Thank *you*," she said. After a moment, "How do we get out of this? It's starting to feel too good."

He laughed loudly, withdrew and flipped her hair with his finger. "You're too much."

"So are you." She laughed and, pushing him out of the way, went out the door.

Miss Wakefield sat nervously in Snapper's waiting room, wringing her hands. Leslie hadn't been sleeping or eating, despite all Miss Wakefield's efforts. Finally she'd put her foot down and insisted that Leslie see a doctor. She couldn't go on like this much longer without seriously injuring her health.

Miss Wakefield's head snapped up as the door opened and Leslie slowly walked out.

Snapper heard Miss Wakefield say, "There now. I don't know if you feel better, but I feel a hundred percent better now that we've seen a doctor." The door closed.

Snapper put his head in his hands. He reviewed everything Leslie had said in that emotionless voice. She was having trouble sleeping. She felt nauseated a lot. She didn't feel like eating, except for every once in a while when she ate a lot of candy. But then she felt nauseated again. She felt incredibly sluggish and didn't want to get out of bed. She felt a bit bloated but couldn't understand it since she was barely eating.

Snapper shook his head. He couldn't believe she was so incredibly naive. Even when he'd asked, in a matter-of-fact tone, if her menstrual cycle was normal, she just shook her head innocently, saying she wasn't sure, she didn't really keep track of it.

Snapper wrote out the instructions for the blood

test he'd told Leslie was to make sure her blood count was normal.

He just hoped Stuart located Brad. Soon.

Laurie's hand trembled when she pulled the envelope out of her mailbox. It bore the publisher's return address. Carefully she opened the letter, skimmed it, threw up her hands, yelled, "Hallelujah!" jumped into her car and sped to Lance's house.

She pushed open the front door, calling, "Lance? Lance? Are you home?" She ran into the living room, out again, into the dining room, the den and into the kitchen. From the back window, she could see the butler and two ladies working in the garden. Where was he? she wondered.

She ran through the rest of the downstairs, through the library, a little study and a sunny breakfast room, wondering what it must feel like to live in such a great big house all alone. He was nowhere in sight.

She'd never been upstairs in his house before, but this was no time to stand on formality, she thought, rushing up the stairs, calling, "Lance? *Lance!*" She opened the first door she came to and breathlessly looked inside. She saw an opulently furnished room with thick, heavy drapes drawn open. In the center of the room stood a very tall, thin lady, who wheeled as Laurie opened the door.

Laurie gasped. The scarf in front of the lady's face was shocking and eerie.

"I—I'm sorry," Laurie stammered, beginning to shut the door. "I was looking for Lance."

"No, wait," said the lady, her voice deep and commanding. "I've been wanting to meet you." She beckoned Laurie into the room with a bony finger, from which sparkled a large diamond ring.

Laurie backed away, saying, "Oh, I really couldn't. . . ."

"Yes, you could, my dear. Please?" The lady gestured toward a chair. "Won't you join me?"

Laurie took a deep breath, then walked cautiously across the thick carpet and sat down on the edge of the chair.

Stuart threw the mail down. He had placed ads in every single publication having to do with the blind. He had run ads in every major newspaper in America, giving Brad's description and offering a reward for any information leading to his whereabouts.

But he had not received a single response.

Chapter Twelve
The Choice

Laurie closed Vanessa's door quietly. She walked down the stairs quietly. But inside, she was seething.

How dare the woman suggest that she wasn't good enough for Lance? The witch was hateful. And that laugh, that wicked laugh when Laurie had said she had no interest in Lance whatsoever, except as a friend. Why, the woman was positively grotesque! Wearing a scarf across her face that matched her outfit. Did she think because it matched that it wasn't grotesque?

And that stupid story about the fire. Laurie didn't believe for a minute that Lance had started the fire, even if it had happened when he was a little boy. He was too smart to do something like that.

Oh, how she hated that woman. She couldn't even believe she was Lance's mother. She was a witch —she'd probably stolen Lance out of a carriage. It was horrible to sit up there spying on everyone. Horrible.

A line from a poem echoed through Laurie's brain: "Will you walk into my parlor? said a spider to a fly." That was just how the whole long interview had felt.

That prying way she had of asking questions about

Europe. The woman was clever, though, Laurie had to admit. Somehow she'd managed to unnerve Laurie, causing her to stammer like a guilty teenager. The woman had made her feel degraded and cheap, when she'd never even done any more than hug Lance. Once.

And just when she'd been feeling so wonderful, so on top of the world about her book. Would she never feel good for more than one minute? Was the world so evil that it would never let her feel anything but shame or torment?

Laurie slammed the front door, not caring if the woman heard. She made a person's skin crawl, thought Laurie, climbing into her car. She was afraid to look up, afraid that horrible woman would be staring down at her from her lair, divining her innermost thoughts. Because it was true. She hadn't admitted it to herself, really, although she'd let the thought drift slowly through her mind.

She started her car and drove down the drive. It was true—she did love Lance. She'd never felt anything like this with anyone else.

She'd only wanted Brad because he was Leslie's. She could admit that, being honest with herself. But even with Mark, as much as she'd loved him, it hadn't ever felt as good as when she was with Lance. No one had ever been able to talk back to her before. And it wasn't just that they had fun together. It was that he seemed to understand her, beneath the surface. He didn't pull back from her and cringe. The best part was that she never felt angry when she was with him. Everyone else always had her hopping mad. They were all such phonies. But with Lance —maybe because they did so much bantering—way down deep inside, she felt peace. A strange, unfamiliar, but incredibly comfortable peace.

She pulled out onto the road. This was terrific, she thought, lighting a cigarette and flooring the car. She had finally found the man she wanted . . . and he had a witch for a mother.

Great.

Vanessa and Lance walked arm in arm along the lake, her head only a few inches lower than his, their long, slow strides evenly matched. From a distance, it was clear by their bone structure and the easy way they moved together that they were mother and son.

They chatted pleasantly. She pointed out which duck was which. They laughed about the names she'd given them. She revealed her plans for the spring. She was going to introduce swans onto the lake, if they'd take to it. She even had a desire to make their property into something of a bird sanctuary and asked Lance if he couldn't call up one of his cronies who handled such matters.

Lance agreed, and they strolled along in pleasant, companionable silence.

"A very interesting thing happened this morning," Vanessa said in the same chatty voice.

"Oh, really, Mother? Did James drop a tray?" Lance asked, looking out across the lake.

"Don't be silly." Vanessa laughed and squeezed his arm. "No, actually, it was something rather out of the ordinary."

"I can't imagine what would be more out of the ordinary than James dropping a tray. I've never seen him drop or spill anything in over twenty years. If I didn't know better, I'd think he was a robot."

Vanessa threw back her head and laughed. Leaning close to Lance, she continued walking, saying, "James comes from very respectable people. Don't forget, his father was a war hero. And you've met his poor old mother on more than one occasion. Robot, indeed." Vanessa laughed again.

Something about his mother's voice and her smug attitude began to ring warning bells in Lance's head. She looked just like a cat who'd caught the canary, the way she was laughing and talking. He glanced at her; her eyes were shining.

"All right, Mother. What happened this morning?"

"I thought you'd *never* ask," she said, turning to him. Through her veil, he could see a smile playing around her lips. He didn't like this. She was being too roundabout and cagey.

"I had a little chat this morning," she said.

Lance slowed his pace. "You had a little chat with whom?"

"Oh, just a little chat," Vanessa said, drawing her fur collar around her neck and pulling him forward.

"You don't *chat* with anyone," said Lance.

Again Vanessa threw back her head and laughed. She gave Lance a sidelong glance. "Not everyone comes bursting into my room, unannounced, uninvited and screaming your name like a stuck pig."

Lance stopped and held Vanessa's arm, but she tugged his gently and began moving them along. "Of course you never even told me her name, let alone introduced us." Vanessa smiled smugly. "But Laurie and I got along famously."

Lance sighed. "I bet you did," he said, looking back out on the lake.

"Aren't you curious about what we had to say to one another?" she asked.

"Not really," Lance answered, not looking at her.

"You're not a good liar, son." Vanessa squeezed his arm. "I know you're consumed with curiosity."

"Think again, Mother."

"Well, I'll just tell you anyway, and you can pretend not to listen. I made it perfectly clear to your little friend that while it was all well and good for the two of you to go traipsing off to Europe, and doing heaven knows what filthy things, she was not welcome in our home."

"You did what?!"

"Ah-hah!" Vanessa laughed, a cold, hard sound. "I knew you'd be interested. Of course, the little devil baldly lied. Said you hadn't slept together. As if I was interested in the intimate details of your seedy little romance."

Lance counted to ten. He knew Vanessa wanted to get his goat. If she suspected for one minute that he cared, he was through. She had managed to break off more than one affair, scaring away several girls Lance would've preferred to stop seeing at his own leisure.

He was surprised at the protective feeling rising in him for Laurie. She was tough, but she wasn't Vanessa's equal. She had several decades less experience, he thought wryly. Suddenly he had a vision of the two of them spitting at each other like cats. It struck him as funny, and he gave a loud, genuine laugh.

Vanessa looked at him, surprised. "You seem to find the whole thing amusing. I'm certainly glad. I was afraid you'd pull a long face." She didn't like this, not one bit.

Lance put his arm around her shoulders and squeezed as he led her along.

"What's gotten into you, Lance?" Vanessa asked nervously.

Lance laughed again. "Actually, Mother, I would've given anything to see the two of you in the same room. I'm surprised the fuses in the house didn't blow."

Vanessa snorted. "She was very tame. All that

bravado slipped down around her ankles and left her stammering and stuttering like a little servant girl who'd been caught trying on one of her mistress's hats."

Lance raised his eyebrows. So, his mother had gotten to Laurie. In a way, he was pleased. It just proved that her toughness was all an act.

They continued to walk, Lance's arm around his mother's shoulder. He was feeling very good.

He realized that his feelings for Laurie were growing. The best part about it was that he felt so easy and free with her. She was the first woman he'd ever known who could actually *talk* to him. Something about her made him feel easy and relaxed. And he felt something unfamiliar with her, something he'd never felt with anyone else. A kind of deep peace. He didn't have to pretend. He could say anything he wanted. With time, he felt sure she'd learn how to deal with Vanessa. In fact, when he thought about it, she was the first woman he'd ever met who had it in her to stand up to his mother. He felt wonderful.

"Lance," Vanessa said, breaking the silence.

"Yes, Mother?" he replied, distracted by his thoughts.

"Lance, I'd really rather you didn't see any more of this Laurie."

"Don't be ridiculous, Mother. I'm a grown man. I'll see whom I please. You know that as well as I."

"Lance." Vanessa stopped and turned to face him. Her eyes were deadly serious, with a depth of feeling that surprised him. She reached up and grabbed his lapels. "Lance I've never said this to you before. But I'm going to say it now. Maybe it's not fair, what I've done to you all these years." Her eyes searched his. "Maybe a mother has no right to demand so much attention from her son. But Lance," she said, her voice impassioned, "you're all I've got in this world."

She saw his eyes soften as he reached out and stroked her hair. "That's not true, Mother. You've got Lucas. We both love you in our own ways."

"Yes, but it's different with Lucas," she said, pleading. "I know he loves me, and I love him. But ever since the fire . . ." She felt Lance stiffen. "No, let me go on," she said, the same intense passion in her eyes and voice. "I'm growing old. I may never have the chance to say this again. Ever since the fire, I've felt bound to you in a way I can't describe. Every mother gives life to every child. But Lance, I gave you life twice. And *I gave you mine*," she cried, tugging on his lapels.

She saw the look in his eyes—of caring mixed with pain—and she went on, trying to control herself. "They say that when one person saves the life of another, that life is theirs to guard forever—more sacred even than their own. It's true, Lance, it's true. Your life is so very, very precious to me," she said fiercely.

"I know, Mother," Lance said, looking into her eyes. She could see the love he felt for her, see it in his eyes.

"I love you," she whispered, "because even as a little boy you were so noble. You admitted you started that fire."

Lance stiffened again.

"No, don't draw away from me, son. I admired you so, admired your innate character."

Lance turned away from her, and she reached up to draw his face back again. "It's all right, son, I know."

"You don't know, Mother," he spat out.

"Oh, but I do." She nodded wisely. "I know that you admitted to something that took guts. I will always love you deeply for that."

Lance turned away.

"Don't shrug it off, son. Not everyone has guts." She paused, then said in a small voice, "I don't have guts."

Lance smiled slightly. "You're not exactly a clinging vine."

"But I am, Lance, I am." She pulled at his lapels, the intense passion back in her voice. "Can't you see that I'm afraid?"

"Afraid?"

"I'm afraid of losing you," she cried. She looked into his eyes with such longing that Lance felt a wave of love rush over him for his mother, who had so little in her life. He reached out and stroked her hair, whispering, "You'll never lose me, Mother. I promise."

"Oh, but I am, I am," she said, tears stinging her eyes. "I can feel it. Lance, please don't make me beg. Please don't make me grovel. I will if I have to, but please don't make me. Blood of my blood, flesh of my flesh, I'm begging you. Lance! Please *give up this girl.*"

Lance was stunned. He always knew she loved him, but he'd never seen this side of her. It tore him inside. He wanted to soothe her.

"Easy, girl," he said in a soothing voice, looking down into her eyes. "You've got the cart before the horse. Nothing's happening between us."

"But that's where you're wrong," she said tearfully. "It is."

Lance turned his face from hers. It was true: it *was* happening. He knew it was happening with the same internal feeling that told him when it was time to shift gears. It was right. Everything about it was right. He knew he wanted Laurie. He wanted to marry her. His eyebrows shot up at the thought. He'd never even considered marriage with anyone before. But yes, it was true. He wanted to marry her. He looked back at his mother.

She stood with her face close to his. He could see the tears trembling in her eyes. He could see the fear there, too. He didn't want to hurt her; she'd been hurt enough in her life. He began shaking his head, feeling his heart sink.

"Please, Lance," she whispered.

He felt tears begin. He couldn't look at her, couldn't bear to see the pain in her face. He kept shaking his head, trying to shake away the pain, not wanting to hurt her. "Mother, Mother," he said, unable to meet her eyes, "please don't force me to make this choice."

"You see?" she cried. "You've already made it."

"Oh, Mother!" Lance threw his arms around her. "Don't do this," he sobbed. "Don't do it to me. Don't do it to yourself."

They embraced, each crying silently. The ducks honked out on the lake. The water softly lapped the shore. Far in the distance, a plane sounded in the air.

Finally Lance murmured in her ear, pleading, "You'll see, Mother. You'll learn to like her. You're a lot alike. Please try, Mother."

Vanessa pulled back from Lance and drew herself up straight. "I will *not* like her, Lance," she said coldly, brushing the tears from her eyes.

His eyes searched hers. He felt so close to her, closer than he'd ever felt. He wanted to hold on to that and reached out to touch her shoulder.

But she pulled away and stood shaking with anger. "I'm giving you fair warning. I will do everything in my power to stop this."

She turned and walked away, her head high, her hands clenched in fists, her eyes dry.

Lance picked up a rock and heaved it into the lake. Then he turned, tears streaming down his face. "Mother!" he called.

But she was gone, and his voice echoed plaintively off the lake.

Lance and Laurie sat side by side on a mound of dirt at the edge of the spur. He had called and asked her to meet him there. He threw a rock, and they watched it bounce along the flat concrete of the road bed.

Laurie sat with her knees drawn up in her arms. Her nose was red. It was cold, even though she was wearing a down jacket and a knitted cap. She knew Lance had something important to say to her from the sound of his voice on the phone, so she sat in the cold, waiting silently for him to speak.

He didn't look at her. Finally he blurted out, "Look, I'm sorry for whatever my mother said."

Laurie didn't answer. What could she say? It had been horrible. She couldn't lie.

He tried again. "I hope she wasn't too hard on you."

She shrugged. "It was nothing a good stiff drink couldn't cure."

"Sometimes she's so . . . so . . ." Lance searched for the word.

"Domineering is what you're looking for, I believe," Laurie said, lighting a cigarette. "Possessive is good, too."

"Well, she's got her reasons."

"Bull," said Laurie, heaving the cigarette out onto the road bed. "She told me that story. My heart bleeds for her. You know what I think? I think it's a crock."

His eyes searched her face. "What do you mean?"

She leaned back on her elbows. "I don't know. I just don't believe you started that fire."

Lance's eyes opened wide. "Why not?"

"I don't know." She shrugged. "I just don't believe it."

Lance sat rolling a rock around between his hands, the muscles in his jaw working. "You know, you're the first person who ever said that," he said, not looking at her.

"Well, did you or didn't you?"

Lance shook his head.

Laurie sat up and looked at his face. His expression was stony. "But why does she think you did?"

He turned away from her and said in a low voice, "I was covering for my brother."

She grabbed his shoulder and turned him toward her. "You were what?"

He turned away. "I was covering for my little brother. He started it. But he lied and said he didn't. So I didn't really say I'd done it. I just said it was true that someone had been playing with matches, thinking he'd admit it then. But he never did."

"So all these years, you've let that lie stand?"

He nodded.

"Why?" she asked with real curiosity.

He shrugged. "I don't even know why. It just seemed right. It seemed like it would be squealing if I said anything."

"Don't you think it's time you told your mother?"

Lance heaved the rock. "What for?"

"The truth, for one thing. It's true that she saved your life. But it's not true that it was your fault." Laurie lay back and rested her head on her arms.

"What difference does it make?" Lance asked, lying down next to her.

"Maybe your little brother could take over in the guilt department after all these years," she said.

"My little brother is not the most noble creature who ever graced this earth," Lance said half to himself.

They lay in silence, looking up at the gray sky.

"So now you know my big secret," Lance said, turning his face toward hers. "What's yours?"

She turned to face him. "Mine?"

"Sure. Everybody's got at least one big secret."

Laurie rolled her eyes. "I've got tons of them."

"No, really," said Lance. "I told you one. Now you tell me."

She turned her face from his and said in an even tone, "I'm a bastard."

Lance laughed. "No, you're a bitch. I'm a bastard."

"I'm serious, Lance."

He sat up and, leaning on his elbow, looked down at her. "What do you mean?"

"Stuart's not my real father."

"How do you know that?"

"I guess my mother ought to know. She's the one who told me. And, of course, swore me to her deep, dark secret."

"Do you know who your real father is?"

Laurie nodded.

"What's he like?"

"He's all right. As respectable as they come."

Lance whistled, shook his head and flopped back down. "We certainly come from fine stock, you and I."

"Yeah. Don't we, though," said Laurie. "Bastions of decency. Pillars of the community."

"Well," Lance said, breathing deeply, "now you know my secret, and I know yours."

"Yup."

"And we both come from fine, upstanding, wholesome families with no skeletons in the closets."

"Yup."

"So I guess there's nothing stopping us, then, is there?" Lance said, still staring up at the sky.

"Nope." Laurie grinned and lay on her back, also looking up at the sky. "Just a couple of formalities."

Lance wiggled his hand into his jeans pocket and pulled out a little box. He tossed it on her stomach.

She picked it up. "What's this, something from a Cracker Jack box?"

"Nah, I didn't spend that much."

"Pretty plain paper," she said, turning the box around in her hand.

He could hear the smile in her voice. "You're such a country bumpkin. That happens to be Tiffany's paper, cretin."

"Oh, fancy, fancy," said Laurie, unwrapping the box. She opened it, and her eyes widened. "Oh, Lance, this is too big."

"You don't like it?" he said, snatching the box and tossing it behind him. Laurie rolled over and started to crawl toward it, but he grabbed her and pulled her on top of him. "Come here, you, he said.

Laurie adjusted her collar nervously. She had dressed very carefully for this meeting with Vanessa, choosing a simple pale pink silk shirt and gray skirt. She wore pearls, and she'd taken off her red nail polish and painted her nails a pale translucent pink. She didn't really feel like herself, but she thought it was important to show respect to Vanessa through her clothes. She just hoped she could get through this without a cigarette.

She tapped lightly at Vanessa's door.

"Come in," came Vanessa's deep voice. Again that line ran through her head: "Will you walk into my parlor? said a spider to a fly." Laurie took a deep breath, put on her most demure smile and peeked her head around the door.

"Stop pussyfooting around and come in here," Vanessa said haughtily.

Laurie sighed; this was not going to be easy. She came into the room, feeling Vanessa's scrutiny as she walked toward the chair the woman indicated.

"I see you've dressed for the occasion," said Vanessa, openly looking her up and down. "It doesn't become you in the least."

So much for clothes, Laurie thought as she carefully placed her hands in her lap and crossed her feet at the ankles.

"And you're not sprawling all over the place like a slut," Vanessa said, and smiled when she saw the quick flash of anger in Laurie's eyes.

"Mrs. Prentiss—"

"The one and only *Mrs.* Prentiss, my dear," Vanessa interrupted.

Laurie held her breath. She would not let this woman get to her. She had come here to make peace. "I've come here today to try and get to know you," she said, feeling as if she had to begin somewhere.

"I see no earthly reason why you should presume to get to know me."

Laurie looked at Vanessa, about to say some other placating sentence. But as their eyes met, the intensity of the anger and hatred coming from Vanessa's eyes twisted something inside Laurie. She felt an equal hatred and fury rise up within her, and suddenly her careful plans of keeping cool flew out the window.

"I came here to make peace with you," she said, rising from her chair and not concealing her anger. "I came here willing to try. But you don't seem to want to try. So let me skip all the amenities and be blunt. Lance and I are going to be married."

"So he has informed me. Care for some tea?" she said, her manner suddenly calm and gracious.

"No, I don't, thank you." Laurie turned to leave.

Vanessa sighed deeply and said, "I suppose I owe you an apology for my lack of manners." At Laurie's look of surprise, she continued, "You can put yourself in my place, can't you? After all, I'm getting on in years. Lance is very dear to me. I think a bit of hostility toward you is understandable, if not polite or generous, wouldn't you agree?"

Laurie looked at her warily. Maybe what Lance had said was true; maybe they really *were* alike. Laurie certainly knew the feeling of being forced to apologize for having said something horrible in a moment of anger. And maybe this wouldn't be so hard. All she had to do was stand up to Vanessa, and the woman would back down.

"What do you say? Shall we put down our dukes and have a real chat?" asked Vanessa. "Please, sit down."

Laurie sat back down, feeling her anger ebb. "I'm sorry I was rude to you. It wasn't nice."

"Oh, but it's perfectly understandable. I dug at you terribly. Inexcusable, really, even for me." She smiled and handed Laurie a cup of tea, then poured another cup for herself and settled back in her chair. "There's one thing in your favor. You seem like a bright young girl. Up until now, my son has shown an appalling lack of taste in women," she said conspiratorially.

Suddenly Laurie found herself warming to Vanessa. She *did* seem to understand her. And maybe she would come to accept her after all.

"But you haven't come here to hear about Lance's exploits, have you? I would imagine, like any young fiancée, you'd prefer to hear some of the stories of Lance's childhood that he's too embarrassed to talk about. Has he told you that he was the champion high-jumper in his sixth-grade class?"

Laurie smiled and settled back in her chair, a wonderful image of little Lance appearing in her mind's eye.

Vanessa's voice took on a faraway sound as she told one amusing anecdote after another, smiling and laughing. Laurie grew more and more comfortable as they laughed and talked. She sensed the true love Vanessa felt for Lance by the way she spoke of him. It was touching, and the picture that emerged of Lance as a child was very engaging.

As the afternoon sun dwindled, the butler came in silently and lit a fire. Vanessa introduced James to Laurie, who refrained from mentioning that they'd already met, then embarrassed him by adding that he was a dear and trusted member of the family. When he'd retired, they sat in companionable silence, drinking another cup of tea as the fire glowed.

Vanessa looked at Laurie, smiling pleasantly. "You know, I said it before, but it's true. You really are the brightest girl Lance has ever been interested in. None of the others have asked such intelligent questions about him."

"I want to know him better. I think you get a good picture of someone when you talk to their mother," Laurie said.

"Yes, I suppose so. I suppose you are genuinely

more interested in him than all the other girls I've had to have this little chat with."

Laurie glanced sharply at Vanessa. Vanessa went on in the same easy tone, "You know, Laurie, I really think we can be friends, you and I. Even after all this has blown over."

"What do you mean?" Laurie said, watching Vanessa's face, barely visible through her scarf.

Vanessa shrugged. "Oh, all the other ones have disappeared as soon as it's been called off. I've never formed an attachment to any of them. There was only one who even had the decency to send a ring back. But of course, she herself came from a very fine family. Most of the others just grabbed their diamonds and ran. Did Lance give you one of his Tiffany specials?" Vanessa said, chuckling.

Laurie felt her anger rising. So, this engagement was nothing more than a fling. Lance was just a playboy with more money than he knew what to do with. Then, abruptly, Laurie's eyes narrowed. "Why, you . . . you . . . conniving witch!" she spat out furiously.

Vanessa just looked at her, the picture of innocence. "I'm not conniving. I've been very frank with you. Ask Lance about all the other so-called engagements. He'll lie, of course. He always has been a bit too skillful at lying for my taste."

"Oh, no, you don't," Laurie said, shaking her head. "You're not going to pull this off. I don't believe you. I don't have to ask him. In fact, I wouldn't dream of asking him. I trust him too much."

"Perhaps you're not as bright as I thought," Vanessa said, sipping her tea.

Laurie hesitated for a moment, a doubt still niggling at her heart. But then she stood. "Let me make one thing perfectly clear. Lance and I are going to be married whether you like it or not."

"Good for you!" Vanessa shook her fist. "Stand up for yourself. There was only one other one who had the guts to say that to me." She slipped her teacup onto the table and said musingly, "What was her name? Oh, well, I suppose it doesn't matter, does it? She's gone, and I'm still here."

Laurie stood where she was, seething. Maybe, she told herself, just maybe the woman was telling the truth.

Vanessa looked regretful. "I'm sorry, Laurie. I really think you and I could be friends."

She watched Laurie's face and was pleased to note the haunting doubts around her eyes. "You're a fighter all right," she said. "Well, I suppose there's nothing for it but to give you the final word, although it sounds so melodramatic. You'll marry him, my dear, over my dead body." She looked at Laurie, gauging her. "Well, I'm sorry, but you'll have to run along now." She began to rise.

Laurie threw back her head and laughed. "You're already dead, and you don't even know it."

Vanessa looked shocked. Laurie was glad, glad to see she'd finally gotten through the woman's cool exterior. "You sit here spying on people, never seeing anyone, and never letting anyone see you. You call that life?" she demanded. "Well, think again, baby."

"How dare you speak to me like that?" Vanessa said, drawing herself up to her full height.

"I'll speak to you any way I damn well please," Laurie said flippantly.

Vanessa pointed to her door, her finger trembling. "Get out of here."

"Oh, I'll get out of here all right. But let me just say one more thing. I came over here wanting to make peace with you." Laurie's voice dripped sarcasm. "I asked Lance a lot of questions, and my heart went out to you, fool that I was. You don't deserve any human feelings. Before I knew what you were really like, I did some research. I brought a little gift for you." She reached into her bag and pulled out a piece of paper, dangling it. "This is the name of the best plastic surgeon in the world. He's in Switzerland. But you won't use it. You'd rather sit up here and scheme and spy. But I'll leave it for you," she said, letting the paper slip out of her fingers onto a small table. "In case you get the guts to face the world." She stared at Vanessa for a moment, then wheeled and slammed out of the room.

Vanessa stood trembling with rage. No one, ever, *ever*, had dared speak to her like that. She looked at the piece of paper lying on the table and took a step toward it.

Her door flew open, and she drew back, shocked.

Laurie shouted in at her, "I'm giving you one month to get this taken care of. That way, you can be at our wedding. But I'm warning you"—Laurie pointed a finger at her—"there's going to be a wedding. Whether you're there or not. Is that clear, *Mrs.* Prentiss?" She slammed the door.

Lance and Laurie stood at the airport window waiting for Vanessa's flight from Switzerland to arrive. Lance was nervous. When the plane arrived, he cupped his hands at the window and watched the passengers disembark. Finally he saw his mother's straight, tall form appear at the top of the gangplank. It was the first time he'd ever seen her form without the fluttering scarf over her face. He watched her say good-bye to the stewardess and regally descend the stairs, her head high.

He reached down and drew Laurie to him. With his hands on both sides of her face, he stared into her eyes. "I can't tell you how much I love you," he said. "I can't thank you enough for what you've done for my mother. You are the most wonderful person I've ever known in my whole life." He kissed her hard, grabbed her hand and ran toward the international arrival gate.

When Vanessa finally emerged from the glass doors, Laurie dropped back. Lance and Vanessa walked toward one another, then both stopped several feet away. They stared at each other.

"Oh, Mother, it's so good to *see* you." Lance ran forward and swept her into his arms, then held her at arm's length and stared at her face. She was smiling brilliantly, and the sight brought tears to his eyes. "Mother," he said, his voice thick, "you're a knock-out."

"I suppose I'll do." She laughed, then looked around her. "Where's Laurie?"

Laurie stepped forward, and they looked at one another shyly. At the same moment they moved forward, exchanged quick, distant hugs and parted.

"I'm sorry I had to be so harsh about it," Laurie said.

Vanessa patted Laurie's cheek. "You're a good girl, my dear. We're going to get on famously." Then she drew both their arms through hers and led them along toward the parking lot. "Now, let's get busy making these wedding arrangements."

Lance had never been happier in his life. He had a woman he loved, someone who could stand up to his mother and who had brought his mother out of her prison.

Laurie had never been happier in her life. She was

in love with the most wonderful man in the world, and her book had been accepted.

Vanessa had never been more frightened in her life. As they walked along, the three of them, arm in arm, she felt exposed, naked and terrified. She wanted this girl out of their lives; she had already made plans. If she could just stall the wedding long enough, she could put a stop to it. Once and for all.

Brad sat on a park bench, his head in his hands, thinking. His money was dwindling. He had learned that Leslie had canceled a big tour—the very thing he'd wanted to avoid more than anything had happened. All his good intentions had been for naught. And now, as he sat in the lonely darkness of day, he wished he could go home. But Leslie didn't want him. He shook his head wearily, felt along the bench for his cane, found it and began tapping his way down the path of the park, his shoulders stooped, his head bowed, his handsome face deeply lined.

Lance hugged Vanessa. "I won't be gone long, Mother. Just a few days."

"That's all right, dear," Vanessa said brightly. "Laurie and I have our hands full planning the wedding."

Lance looked her in the eye and shook his head. "No, Mother. Laurie's coming with me."

Vanessa felt her heart stop. "But Lance, there's so much to attend to."

He shook his head and said simply, "I'm sorry, Mother. I didn't want it this way." He turned.

"Lance," she called, her hand outstretched as the door closed.

* * *

The street blazed white hot. Neon signs glared.

"But why are we in Las Vegas?" Laurie asked as Lance hustled her along by the elbow. "I thought you had one of your muckety-muck business meetings, and I was just supposed to tag along and be beautiful until the evening."

Hank followed them, taking long easy strides, his eyes crinkling as he smiled.

"This *is* business. Serious business," Lance said grimly as he led her toward a office building that bore a small plaque: JUSTICE OF THE PEACE.

Laurie stopped dead in her tracks, squinting up at him in the sun. "Hold it. Hold it right here. Suppose you tell me what's going on."

Lance pushed his sunglasses up on top of his head. "I couldn't figure out why Mother was busy making such long, involved wedding arrangements—until I heard her whispering into the phone. She hired a private detective to find out something on you."

"Are you kidding?" Laurie asked, stunned.

"Nope," Lance said. "I wish I were."

"But there's nothing to find out!" Laurie protested.

"You think I'm willing to risk that?" he said, grabbing her elbow.

"Just a damn minute." She pulled her elbow out of his hand. "If you think there's something in my past that you don't want to know about . . ."

"I'm just teasing you," he said, smiling. Then his smile faded. "I'm just so furious with Mother I could spit. We tried to be nice. We wanted her at the wedding. I don't want to play her games anymore. Besides, a wedding is really just between two people anyway, when it's all said and done. Now shut up, and let's go." He hustled her in through the door, and the air conditioning hit them.

"Lance, slow down for a minute."

Lance could see Laurie was serious. He turned to Hank. "You want to beat it for a minute? Go down there and take care of paperwork."

Hank ambled down the hall, shaking his head and mumbling, "You two."

They stood in the dingy hall, light from a single fluorescent tube reflecting forlornly off the institutional-green walls. It was one of the least romantic spots in the world, but neither of them noticed.

"Lance," Laurie began, her face strained. "Can I ask you something?"

"Sure." He smiled.

"Lance . . . " She stopped and stomped her foot. "Lance, *please* can I have a cigarette?"

"No. The mother of my children does not smoke. Next question."

She fumbled in her pocket and brought out a mint, stuck it in her mouth and took a deep breath. "Now, I want to ask you something that's hard. Something we once agreed never to talk about."

Lance looked at her. She was having trouble meeting his eye. In a flash, as if he'd read her mind, he knew what she was asking. Laughing, he shook his head, put his hands on her shoulders and looked her in the eye. "I'm only going to say this once, so listen up. I have known *lots* of other women. I have felt lots of things for them."

Tears stung her eyes. Laughingly, lovingly, he said, "It's just quitting smoking. You're doing great. Now let me finish. I have never asked another woman to marry me."

She searched his eyes. Somehow it wasn't enough. She had to know. Maybe it wasn't nice, but she *had* to know.

He pointed a finger at her nose. "Now I mean this,

Laurie. I'm only going to say this once in a long, long life together. And I'm only going to say it at all because you need to hear it. But it goes against my grain as a gentleman." He paused. "I never loved Leslie the way I love you."

She looked at him; one tear spilled over. He wiped it away and continued gently, "You're special to me. More special than anyone in the whole world. I know things haven't always been easy with you and your family. I know you've never really felt loved."

She looked at him, surprised. "How do you know that?"

He put his finger on her lip, silencing her. "I know everything about you. I know sometimes you're not nice." Her eyes darted, and he laughed. "I know everything there is to know about you. I still want you. I want you to be my wife."

Tears streamed down her face. As he wiped them away, he leaned down to kiss her. "Okay?" he said softly.

She nodded.

He drew her arm through his, and together they walked toward the office.

"But Lance," she said.

"What *is* it?"

"I'm not dressed."

"What do you call those jeans? Now shut up."

The ceremony was short. Hank and the office secretary stood as witnesses. When it was over, Lance took Laurie's face in his hands and kissed her, a long, hungry, loving kiss that she returned.

They broke apart. "How does it feel to be married to one of America's wealthiest industrialists?" he asked, smiling into her eyes.

"I don't know," she answered, laughing. "I think

there's something married people are supposed to do that we haven't done yet."

He swept her up in his arms and strode out the door, calling over his shoulder to Hank, "Get lost for three days."

As he strode down the street in the blazing sun, Laurie clung to him, bouncing along in his arms, laughing and crying. He kicked open the door of the first hotel he passed and hollered, "Give me a room for me and my wife. And hurry up. I'm sweating like a pig. She's heavy for a little thing."

Laurie laughed. The clerk laughed. The bellhop ran, grabbed a key, led them into a room on the first floor and stood there.

"Get lost," Lance said. "I'll tip you later."

He looked down into Laurie's eyes, carried her over the threshold and kicked the door shut behind them.

Jennifer was awakened by Stuart's tossing and turning. Obviously, he was finding it hard to sleep. *Oh Stuart*, she thought, *you can't go on searching for Brad Elliot forever. He obviously doesn't want to be found.* She didn't say it aloud. Not for fear she would wake Stuart—she knew he was awake—but because she knew he would only dismiss her opinion, as he had so many times before. Gently placing her hand on his arm, Jennifer tried to reassure him that she was there for him if he wanted to talk.

Stuart responded to her touch. "I'm sorry, Jen. I can't seem to sleep." He was contrite.

Jennifer smiled and made light of it all. "What say I go downstairs and get us both a glass of warm milk? It worked wonders for Chris when she was a baby." Stuart protested that he was not a baby, but Jennifer waved away his complaints and slipped out the bedroom door.

As she reached the kitchen, her thoughts were riveted inward as she tried to decipher the terrible feeling that was creeping over her. Suddenly, she grabbed the kitchen counter to steady her swaying form. She felt sick—terribly sick. Just as swiftly as the feeling had overtaken her, Jennifer was well again.

Taking a deep breath, she shook off fears that she was seriously ill. But, a little voice inside told her that she was. She vowed to say nothing to Stuart. She needed time to find out what was wrong.

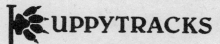